WHO
WILL I BE WITH
IN HEAVEN?

A Graphic Tale of Life and the Afterlife

JORGEA HERNANDO
with PAUL DANNER

Printed in the United States of America
First Printing, 2019
ISBN: 978-1-54398-106-3 eBook 978-1-54398-107-0

IN HONOR OF
MY SUPERHERO

ACKNOWLEDGMENTS

My sincere gratitude to Paul Danner for accompanying me in this journey. He and I wrote the original version of *Who Will I Be With In Heaven?* as a film screenplay in 2011.

Besides been a consummate writer, Paul is a devoted family man. His wife Cheryl, his children, Sophie and Bryson, his mom, Mary Ann, are all supportive and proud of his involvement in our "book"

As we started to convert the script to a novel, in January 2019, new inspirations were generated from the original story. We found out there were an unlimited number of "tales" that we could incorporate into the novel.

My gratitude to KOKO (koko.0adva@gmail.com) for the illustrations and Calum McGhee (cmcgheeillustration@hotmail.com) for the drawings that can be found illustrating the stories within this book. Representing visually what we had in our minds wasn't easy, but they definitely managed to give life to our ideas.

To Image Credits: Shutterstock, National Aeronautics and Space Administration (NASA), Wikipedia Commons (creative commons.org), and Eduardo Hernando (Ride, 2019).

To George, for making me realize the beautiful mission of caring for the elderly.

To Peter, for his huge impact on our family, especially for being friend and mentor to my children Ed and Jorge. His smile, energy, and love for life will forever be remembered.

To my assistant Milton, loyal as family, for his sharp eyes and detailed scrutiny.

To my wife Gladys, my lifetime Dynamo and my children, Jorge, Ed, Carmen, and Gladys-Katherina, who helped organize the book, for the encouragement to start the process of rewriting the script as a novel.

And to my Superhero who makes everything possible.

– Jorgea Hernando

PROLOGUE

Heaven, the most unknown, unpredictable, and mysterious place for the human mind. How do you imagine it? What do you think is there? Well, let me show you...

This is a disco.

Colors flare and flicker in a bright cascade of illumination that washes over a dance floor and its surrounding walls.

A bearded man dressed in a white robe sits inside a DJ booth with studio microphones and equipment ranging from an old analog twenty-four-track tape deck to a laptop computer and modern mixing console.

There are two chairs; the bearded man is seated in one, but as the scene comes into focus, it's clear that he's not a DJ.

He is a Judge. He is open and direct, but with a twinkle of mischief in his eye, talking to a woman sitting in front of him.

"The Lord loves everyone equally, no matter what circumstances they may find themselves."

"I loved Him, too, sir. He is my Savior."

"Yes, but for most of your life, you disregarded God's love with your actions. Despite your acceptance of Him in your heart and abiding to his guidance, you did not take Him with you to the goal line."

"I am sorry. I did a lot of good for others. Give me one more chance to prove I am a good woman worthy of everlasting life!"

"I have made my decision. You do not have a choice. You must take the elevator down." With that statement, he reaches for his cell phone.

"Who are you calling now?

The Judge is done with the conversation. "Push the button down." He turns his attention to the phone call. "Fate, I need to step out for a moment. I'm going to listen to some live music for a change."

I love Los Angeles.

I always have.

The tall palm trees lining the streets and the broad mountain ranges coupled with the cool weather constantly remind me that it is a desert. Its range of neighborhoods and economic classes gives the city a diversity that is unlike other places. Its polarities also carry with it the essence of life. So many different types of people living side by side. There are always so many things to do here, one could occupy themselves every hour of the day. I imagine myself coming here more often . . . But I shake the thought, as I also love peace and quiet.

It seems the car is the mode for that here. In such a sprawling metropolis, the requirement to have a car seems to give people a respite from the hustle and bustle. They lock themselves into their little motorized vehicles and navigate across miles. I've heard that they become pod-like or bubbles in which to momentarily isolate themselves from the millions of others surrounding them.

My preference is to move through the city as an independent entity. I am able to interact with the humans and the details of their lives as I pass by, unbeknownst to them. Today, as I arrive in Los Angeles, my priority is to find music, my favorite activity, and to see as many people as possible, perhaps I might be able to find something worthy of my participation.

My first stop is the unique locale of the Venice Beach boardwalk. I love looking at the picturesque landscape of the ocean with the Santa Monica Mountains in the background. There are few places where the two coexist in such peaceful proximity. On the boardwalk, with its long and wide pedestrian pathway adjacent to miles of sand and the Pacific Ocean and eccentric shops and restaurants, I know it is one of the best places to find local musicians. They perform on the street, the wide variety of people that I enjoy to find in one place. A young couple is playing classic rock over there, but it is the sound of a violin that draws me to a group of tourists huddled in front of a young man in his thirties standing dressed in a suit with his beat-up violin in hand. He is playing a classical tune of which I am not familiar. I search to find the kind of notes that speak to my soul, relax me, and let every note flow though me.

The player's violin case is open in front of him, a gesture welcoming tips from the audience for his talent. Although only a few coins and one or two bills lay scattered in the case, the violin player enthusiastically plays, hoping to inspire a few more tips. An older woman drops some spare change into the case. The violinist displays an appreciative smile and continues to play.

I notice a strange-looking man standing in the crowd. He appears to be scanning the crowd, possibly looking for someone or something. I keep my eyes on him, seeing his next move. Suddenly, he steps into the crowd, standing close to a young woman, and attempts to pick-pocket the wallet from her purse.

"This won't do . . ." I murmur.

Right before the pick-pocket can get his hands on the wallet, the woman reaches back to put her hand in her purse. The pick-pocket retreats from his target, clearly startled that the woman almost grazed his hand as she reached into her bag. Unaware of the man, the woman pulls out a handful of change and walks to the open violin case, dropping in her coins. Deciding against his earlier intentions, the pick-pocket finally walks away, clearly upset about his failed attempt.

Choices, choices, choices, I think as I listen to the tunes of the violin. As he finishes his song, the violin performer bows to the crowd before him, then readies the violin beneath his chin for his next song. A hefty breeze blows over the crowd from the cresting ocean as I turn to continue my journey.

With the sound of the strings in my mind, I continue to walk down the boardwalk, observing the people and activities going on around me. I notice the architecture of the buildings; how different the structures are from one another. The rounded corners and long stretches of concrete slabs, the new buildings like square blocks, Mediterranean-style houses with terra-cotta roof tiles, and other old places with ugly stucco walls collide to reflect the diversity of Los Angeles itself.

After a few blocks, I turn onto a busy street and sense something amiss. A red Jaguar is speeding in my direction, out of control, and its driver in clear distress. The brakes don't seem to be working. I can see the man inside struggling to stop the car without brakes. He will surely run the red traffic light.

Erratically honking the horn, the driver swerves around the cars stopped at the light, almost losing complete control. Pedestrians on the sidewalk stop to look at the scene, covering their mouths in anticipation of what will happen next.

As the car speeds past the red light, a young woman gets ready to cross the road. She does not see the car speeding her way. She appears lost in thought! There is simply no time to warn her. By the time the car speeds past her, the woman will be in the middle of the crosswalk at exactly the same . . . the car will run her over! There is no time.

At that moment, the woman trips on the curb of the pavement and stumbles to the ground, still on the sidewalk. A frustrated look crosses her face as she stands up, looks at the coffee stain on her white shirt, and steps to put her high-heeled shoe back onto her foot. Hot coffee spills over her hand and onto the pavement. Finally hearing the blaring horn, she looks up and sees the red Jaguar speeding past. Her eyes widen in surprise.

In his last attempt, the driver of the speeding car comes to a screeching halt on the side of the road. His face is filled with fear and confusion as he stumbles out of the car, breathing heavily. He stands there as if stoned, trying to make sense of what happened. He looks up and sees the bystanders on the sidewalk start to slowly walk away. He spots the woman standing at the crosswalk, staring at him as she brushes the stain from her shirt. She shakes her head at him then hurls the coffee cup into the trash before stomping to the other side of the road, still complaining about falling and getting her clothing stained. Most people don't realize that sometimes things happen for the best.

We generally don't interfere with people's free will, even if they are going to commit a crime, hurt themselves or others, and even if their acts work against God's fundamental principles. Only when we are directed by the Boss himself do we intervene, usually from the effect of intense prayer or genuine intentions are we allowed to change the course of someone's life, even if they might go back to their immoral habits. If it's not me, one of us deals with them when they reach the end of the line. One of the members of our team welcomes them into whatever path will be laid for them.

Speaking of teams . . . I glide over the busy freeways and street traffic, millions of lights from a million cars create the scene as I arrive at Dodgers Stadium to catch the last part of a baseball game. I can hear the sounds of cheering fans and the Dodgers' announcer calling the game from someone's handheld radio as I move up the hill to the stadium. I walk to the entryway of the grand old stadium, through its open-air passageways and down into the bleachers. The stadium is packed, and only a few seats remain unoccupied. I glance at the scoreboard. The Dodgers are losing at the bottom of the ninth inning and they have one last chance to score. On the field the Dodgers have two men on base; one on third base, another on second, and a man at home plate. With two outs, it does not look like the home team will take this win. I can see the desperation in the players' faces and in the faces of the devout fans.

A quick glance across the stadium shows me that every single heart is busy silently praying, some willing to beg for a near miracle for a Dodgers' win. The anticipation and adrenaline are palpable. Every eye in the stadium is on the field. Everybody is waiting for the final move.

The hitter at the home plate gets ready. For a few seconds, everybody holds their breath, even the players. Then, the pitcher releases the ball with a swift flick of his hand, sends the ball hurtling towards the hitter. It's going to be an easy fly ball.

It feels as if the ball floats slowly in the air for a long time, but in only a split second, the ball connects with the hitter's bat, and it flies towards left field. A huge "Oh . . .!" resonates across the crowd as the fans watch in awe, some standing and readying to leave, others with their eyes frozen on the ball.

Let me make the home team and the people in the stadium happy for a change, I think.

As the outfielder goes to catch the ball, he thinks it will be an easy catch; a great way to end the game and take the win. With that thought, he loses his concentration on the ball coming his way and, in an instant, drops the ball.

Suddenly coming to life, the players on third and second round the bases to score and the Dodgers win the game.

As I watch the home team making their approach to the catcher's box, the woman sitting next to me, along with everybody else, jumps up and shouts, "What a miracle!"

I smile at her comment.

Back on the field, I look at the sheer happiness on the players' faces as they run to each other, hugging and cheering. Their moment of glory is one that spreads to the crowd. I love seeing people happy. It fascinates me to see people sharing a moment of pure happiness with each other. Tomorrow, the front page of the *Los Angeles Times* will feature the headline: "A Miracle Win for the Dodgers."

As I exit the stadium and walk around the nearby neighborhood of Echo Park, I come across an older man, dressed like an office drone, sitting behind the wheel of an expensive and flashy car. He is busy texting on his phone like a fourteen-year-old girl. Preoccupied with the message he is trying to send; he steers the car with his knees as he exits the parking lot. At the stop sign, he barely looks left or right before moving off again into the speeding traffic. Suddenly, the air is filled with the screeching of tires and the irate honking of a car horn. Before the man can so much as react, he looks up at the car speeding his way and realizes he has just violated this driver's right-of-way. It looks like the car will not be able to stop in time. Shutting his eyes, bracing for the unavoidable impact, he readies himself for a nasty broadside crash. A shrill yell fills his ears . . . the cars crash into one another right before my eyes.

My attention falls on a person sitting off-set, a man who seems clearly irritated by something of which I cannot tell. There are people surrounding him and standing on their marks on the set.

"Cut!" shouts James, while he shifts his baseball cap from back to front.

I am on a movie set. This is Hollywood. There are movie sets everywhere. This is the movie-making destination. Like the old song goes, like Doris Day used to sing . . ." Hooray for Hollywood!" The city of the stars and of the ones who want to be stars.

From his director's chair, James shakes his head. His baseball hat blocks his eyes from the morning light as his face becomes serious. He demands the best from his actors and is unforgiving in his demands. A small mistake is reason enough for him to completely reshoot entire scenes, and this time is no exception.

From around a camera rig, Rick, a tall, surly looking man motions with his hands for another take and says, "Again, Jimbo?"

At that moment, James reaches into his pocket for his ringing phone and blankly stares at the scrolling text on the screen, announcing a call from Sage. He takes a deep breath and sighs before silencing the phone and putting it away. He rises from his chair and begins walking towards another camera rig to re-watch the last shot. Rick hurries to catch up to him.

"I don't think I will use any of these shots. This collision scene is predictable, and frankly, it's cliché," James remarks as he stares at the raw footage playing back on the screen.

I tend to agree with him. Many human beings find the tragedy of loss to be somehow entertaining, making blockbuster movies full of blood, gore, and death, then wondering why society seems to replicate similar atrocities. There are statistics showing that horror genre movies have rapidly increased in number since the late twentieth century, alongside horrors across the globe…

Rick responds, "Unless you *are* the accident."

James glances distractedly away, his mind trying to problem-solve the active scene at hand. "What if it's a truck instead? Full of chemicals . . ." He spreads his hands to motion the picture he sees in front of him, one hand gesturing movement simultaneous to the other hand. "Can you picture it?" he asks as he stares into the distance.

From my outsider's perspective, it is difficult for me to understand the need for every movie to end in chaos and destruction, but such is the way of human life.

As I observe James from this distance, I can peer into his intellect, I can behold his brain at work visualizing his new scene. Early morning on a congested road, an eighteen-wheeler truck carrying hazardous materials rockets towards the protagonist, promising fiery doom.

Rick notices James's glassy eyes staring blankly then starts, "Well, that will set us back at least a week."

James turns to focus on the set again, "Make it happen."

Rick motions to the crew and begins a set of directives towards them. "Full rewrite of the last scene. Everyone gathers around for new production requirements."

Simultaneously, the lights begin to flicker off and on as the crew shuts down the stage.

"Wait. Stop. These lights . . . keep them there." Hands on his hips, James notices the exact kind of dim atmosphere that begets the first vestiges of dawn. He imagines large cumulous clouds as he regards the sky above, "Like I can see all the way up to . . ." before pausing with his head tilted upwards.

Here is a moment where I find the opportunity to add a subtle vision to his mind, while it is open in both thought and imagination.

I close my eyes and momentarily focus on his inner being, his light. I nudge him with a vision of a dark room lit by a single candle. The room is empty except for a twin-size bed and a side table with a chair. Gently his mind whispers to him, "James, your life is a wreck."

I utter the words into his subconscious mind, just loud enough for him to take note of the tiny voice confirming what he already knows. James lets out a deep sigh and turns his gaze back to Rick, who is waving a cell phone in his direction.

"Sage sent me a message. She wants you to call her."

"I don't know. I can't think about that now."

"What should I say?"

"Nothing. I've had enough of her lately."

"How can you be tired of Sage? She's the hottest woman you've ever dated," Rick pauses, "after Kate, of course." And he grins.

James gives Rick a curious look. "I'm just tired of her crap, and my own filthy crap. It's a meaningless relationship at this point. I don't want to be that person anymore. Just tell her that I'm busy."

James watches Rick as he unloads a series of texts at Sage. "Why is she texting you anyway?"

"Apparently it's because you never answer," Rick replies.

James rubs his face and yawns. I can sense his exhaustion. Come to think of it, I would feel equally exhausted if I had the same pressure he holds resting on my shoulders. The chaos of his life is only beginning to become apparent to him. Its outcome is so far beyond his hands at this point.

James finally exhales his thoughts, returning to the present, "God, I need some coffee."

As they walk through the lot, an extra lean against the side of a car preparing to take a sip of his coffee. Rick quickly glides up to the man snatching the coffee cup from his hands and passes it to James. The label reads "Apollo's."

I immediately nudge another vision towards James of an Apollo's coffee house. This place is particularly potent for James, "I hate Apollo's," he says as he dumps the cup into the garbage can.

Rick looks at James, "Are you okay? It seems like something other than the picture is on your mind."

James pauses before answering him. "I have an uneasy feeling today."

"What is making you uneasy?"

"I don't know. Just . . . I just feel strange—It's been a long week." Trying to change the subject. "Are we shooting on Saturday?"

"Whitney prefers that we do, but the crew is expecting a long weekend," Rick answers. "So was I."

"Then that's what we're going to do."

Rick begins to suggest, "What about—" as he claps his hand onto his friend's shoulder.

"Don't sweat it. I'll take the brunt of Hurricane Whitney. She's a great producer, but she cracks the whip a little too much sometimes. We can't put such a strain on the crew. Come on, let's go grab breakfast. Take your mind off things."

I follow James and Rick to the craft services table where they are piling eggs, toast, sausage, and pancakes high onto their plates. The two men have clearly been friends since they were boys, it is apparent in their gestures and level of comfort towards one another.

"It really feels like we've been doing this forever," says Rick.

James laughs while crunching on a piece of bacon, "That's because we have."

Rick smacks his arm as they walk to a nearby picnic table, "Man, remember our first series of films in school? We had some great times," Rick says, reminiscing.

"Guerrilla filmmaking, dodging that campus cop douche bag . . . What was his name . . . Sam . . . Steven . . .?"

"Shephard, maybe?"

Shaking his head, Rick replies, "Ah, the days when we didn't have to worry about budgets or demanding producers."

"I'll tell Whitney that we need the weekend off. And more money for special effects."

Rick looks at James. "Seriously? Do you want to die young?"

"I only—" James starts to aggressively cough; he is choking on his food. A burning sensation fills his throat, and his eyes fill with water. He grasps at his neck.

"Are you okay, man?!"

James rapidly shakes his head, trying to cough or breathe, but he cannot even think straight. He can feel the last bits of saliva disappear from his mouth into a parched, dry cavern of esophagus. His face is red and quickly turning blue . . .

James thinks back to the day when he surprised his young lady friend Kate with a sunflower while she studied on their college campus. He watches as the large sunflower bloom leaves his hand and an enormous smile crosses Kate's darling face. His heart is filled with love. It is in that moment that he knows that she is the one.

I know this smidge of memory will ease him into slowly breathing again. It is not yet time for him to meet my dear friend Fate, and so I intervene.

Rick momentarily scrambles to shout for help before getting up to help James with his amateur understanding of the Heimlich Maneuver.

James clutches at his throat, breathing heavily, wiping tears from his face. He wipes his forehead with the sleeve of his shirt, barely smiling. He reaches for a glass of water and heavily gulps it down like a man trapped in a desert.

Rick puts his hand on James's shoulder, saying, "Relax, breath bro."

James feels as if his head is spinning. He could have dropped dead right then and there. "I'm fine. I'm fine." Then, "Wow."

"Yeah. That was close," Rick says.

A few minutes pass in silence. James contemplates, "I'm going to talk to Whitney now."

"Go get her, James!" Following him, Rick adds quietly, "Please don't get us fired."

As he crosses the stage lot towards the parking lot, James notices a nearby commotion. He veers off the path to investigate, still gently stroking his neck.

I stay behind him as he walks past a casting trailer where a young but arrogant production assistant is unnecessarily shouting at a woman with her young son. He looks about nine or ten years old. The boy, clearly in distress, is close to tears.

"Listen, lady, it's not 'bring your kid to work' day," says the irritated man with a scowl on his face.

Hesitantly the woman says, "All he wants is to meet Mr. Glass. His dream is to be a director. I was hoping he could . . ."

"Lady, you're just an extra. Your job is to be seen and not heard," the assistant says, stepping closer to her. The boy flinches at the man, gently tucking his face near his mother's arm. "Well, that *was* your job. You are fired," the man says as he slinks onto the heels of his feet and smiles.

James walks over to the young assistant and says, "The kid stays in the picture."

"Mr. Glass." The man says, surprised. "I'm sorry. This lady brought her son today and . . ."

He turns to the production assistant and says, "You be nice." The man lowers his head to apologize then walks away.

James kneels down, looking into the boy's eyes. "Hey there, I'm James. Do you like movies?"

The kid shyly nods. "I love your movies. I want to be a director just like you."

James mind is suddenly clear. "Really?" he says. "You know what helps me? My director's hat." He fondly smiles as he removes his baseball cap, slapping it lightly onto the boy's head.

"How about a tour of the set? I can have my assistant take you around," James starts.

He begins to envision the boy years into the future, now on his own movie set, still wearing the frayed and worn baseball that James gave him, directing his first film.

"I have an old Super-8 camera. I make superhero movies. It was my mom's."

"We all got to start somewhere, kid. My first tries were tough, but that's how you learn."

The boy and his mom are amazed. But I need to get back to my official duties, so I contact my own assistant, "I am ready, Fate. Send the next one."

* * *

All you can see at first is white smoke; then, the same as before, lights, dance floor, and there he is.

The Judge is listening to music with his audio phones over his ears before he takes them off to speak to the man standing in front of him.

"Hello, Peter, I have been waiting for you," he says.

"Thank you, sir. I am concerned about leaving all my documents totally disorganized. I know my wife will have a hard time getting everything in order; I came too soon.

"At ease, Peter. She will enjoy it, and you came right on your time. Besides, you don't need to be standing so straight as if you are in front of an Air Force superior. Have a seat and let's get started."

"You are a superior, sir, and if you command me to sit down, I will."

Peter walks over to the chair by the table closest to him. The Judge sits down in a chair to his side.

"Tell me seven important moments of your life. Moments that impacted who you are."

"Many of the important moments in my life are classified information, sir. God, family, and country have been my passion and I have a problem talking about what I promised to keep secret."

"Peter, I value your attitude, but here you no longer have to keep secrets. You have to convince me that the majority of your actions are deserving enough for you to decide who you want to be with in Heaven. If one of those secrets moments is the one that makes the difference, you need to tell me about it," says the Judge.

"I understand, sir. I hope I have done enough good for God, my family, and to others that I don't need to talk about my glorious moments serving my country."

"Alright then, go ahead, Colonel Peter."

"I was born in Guantanamo, Cuba, a small city about forty miles from the United States naval base at Guantanamo Bay. My father, a labor leader and revolutionary, was jailed as a political prisoner in the regime of Fidel Castro."

Peter continues, "When I was twenty years old and a student at the University of Oriente, Santiago in Cuba, I had just come back from running and had begun to study in the college library. I was concentrating on the book I was reading when I heard a voice tell me, "Pedro, we are leaving Cuba tonight." It was my father, and I could not believe he was in front of me, because he was in prison. He had tricked the guards, and they let him have one day of leave. But he had spent a lot of time behind bars and had managed to contact some friends outside to have everything organized and only needed a few hours to escape. I didn't hesitate. We went to the car that was waiting and picked up our sisters, Magaly and Telma, and my brother-in-law, Pepin. We drove toward an area where there were railroad tracks. A train came in and hardly stopped, but we climbed inside the boxcar carrying sugar cane and rode inside until it approached the US naval base at Guantanamo, and we jumped from the moving train. We waded waist-deep through a snake-infested swamp before reaching a tall security fence topped with barbed wire. I carried Telmita on my back over the fence and then a second fence inside the perimeter of the naval base. I think because I carried her on my back while we were escaping, Telmita became like the 'married nun' for her spiritual closeness with me."

"International law requires that when an enemy soldier raises his hands in surrender, he will be respected and his dignity maintained, even in a prison. The same principle of respect applies to a person arriving to another country by any means and requesting asylum."

"After we were picked up by US forces, we asked for political asylum. We were taken into custody where we were all given showers, clean clothes, and some food. Soon after, we were each individually interviewed to determine if our situation in Cuba entitled us to asylum in the US. It was a time of concern and stress, but in the end, we succeeded, and the Chief of Naval Operations gave us a ride to Miami in his plane. "

"As I took my first steps in the USA, my heart and soul were filled with joy beyond belief."

"That's a story of courage and determination, Colonel Peter," says the Judge.

"Yes, sir. Father Pastor, my mentor in Guantanamo, told me that if God gives you a lot of talent and blessings, your responsibilities are greater than those without Father Pastor was correct, I wish more talented people would follow that principle."

Peter shifts in his seat, eager to continue. "A few years later, I fell in love forever with my wife Alexandra, and we had two wonderful children, Peter and Amy. They were my life. I very much enjoyed my family and my extended family of cousins, Gladys and her two sons, Eduardo and Jorge.

They were my pride. We had a great time together. I became their mentor. Eduardo and I went several times to Honduras to bring shoes to kids and some adults in need. We were impressed by the gratitude in those people's eyes when they started trying the shoes. They wanted so much to find the right size that would fit them. It was like there were many 'Cinderellas' at the same time," Peter laughs, fondly recalling the moment.

"We wanted to keep going back and enjoyed their happiness. We wondered why the rich and powerful countries, didn't help with funds and training to raise the standard of living in these poor countries."

"My life was full of devotion to God and my family, and I became a Colonel in the United States Air Force. I managed a joint NASA-Defense Department project to build a 1,000-pound experimental spacecraft to go to the moon. The project, known as Clementine, took less than two years from concept to launchpad. I enjoyed it very much because I loved to take on things that seemed impossible."

"Clementine went into space and sent back millions of images of the moon. It measured reflected light and radiation, created a topologic map of the lunar surface, and discovered evidence of frozen water in craters at the moon's south pole."

"After Clementine, I went to work at the National Reconnaissance Office, an agency that no one knew existed for many years. There I helped design and manage spy satellites. But I became bored and left and went to work in the private sector. But, not for long, after the tragedy of the September 11 attacks on the World Trade Center in New York, I was needed back at the National Reconnaissance Office to do some special project. And sir, I'd rather not continue talking about this project. May I stop?"

"No, Colonel Peter, there are no secrets here, keep telling me the stories of your heart and please . . . do not make them like a military briefing."

Very well sir, from my heart, "the moment I met Alexandra..."; Peter continues...

* * *

In Los Angeles, on a busy city street where rush hour is coming to an end, we find a woman and a teenage girl in one of the cars on the road.

Kate's hair is pulled back into a ponytail, and the frown she wears on her brow speaks volumes about where she is about to go. For a woman of her age, she has had her fair share of problems over the years, and in her mind, she was about to drive into yet another problem.

Kate and James's daughter, Jenna Lynn, is in the passenger seat. She seems annoyed. Although merely seventeen years old, Jenna had success thrown at her feet, with a father in the movie industry, and she has done her best to exploit his fame to her favor.

An oil painting of the sea rests in the back seat.

Jenna speaks up, "Thanks again for driving me, Mom. I know this isn't exactly your favorite place to go."

Kate gives her daughter a wry smile. "Why do you say that? I love the magic of the movies . . . Only two hours to a happy ending."

Jenna Lynn looks out the window, her face obviously a little sad. "Too bad that never really happens."

Kate notices the sadness in her daughter's voice and says, "You're too young to be jaded about life."

"Hello? I'm in the recording industry," she replies.

Kate pauses for a moment before responding. "I'm sorry I don't have the money to give you myself."

"No worries. James has deep pockets."

Kate gives her a sideways glance. "Jenna, you only make time to see your father when you need something. It isn't right."

Jenna pauses for a moment to think. "Yeah, well . . . It isn't right what he did to us either. Besides, now that I'm spending so much time in the city, I need a place to stay."

"A place to stay is one thing. A studio with a view of Central Park might be a little much."

"You sure blew that opportunity. I could've been on MTV years ago!" Jenna says with a shrug.

Kate glances over at her daughter and starts to say something but stops, and just keeps driving as the movie set comes into view.

* * *

Back at the Disco, Peter just finished with the seven moments. He looks confident, waiting for the Judge's statement. The Judge looks at Peter's face with a smile and says, "Colonel Peter, you have been a servant of God, family, and the country that adopted you in a very extraordinary way. You deserve to select who will be with you in Heaven."

"Oh, sir, I would love to be with my father, my mother, Pepin, and Pepincito. I'd like to wait with them until the time when I will have my wife with me."

"Colonel Peter, take the elevator up. It will take you to your destiny where your loved ones are waiting for you," says the Judge with a peaceful grin.

"Thank you, sir. Will there be 'leche condensada' where I am going?"

21

"Yes, Peter, condensed milk, cakes, and anything else you could ever want or imagine."

Peter gets into the elevator and pushes the button up.

The Judge picks up his cell and says, "Fate, please send me the next one, this one was easy. I am ready."

The Judge walks over to the console and reviews the different music he has prepared. He is attempting to set his audio phones on his ears, but he stops when a man dressed like a preacher approaches him.

The man looks at the back of his hand to see the number thirty stamped on it.

"Where am I?" the preacher asks.

"Right where you need to be," the Judge replies.

"Am I in Heaven?"

"No."

"I am a servant of God. Don't I go to Heaven automatically?"

"I do not know. You were set on a path, but you are given free will to make choices. The question is if your choices were as pious as your faith." The Judge pauses. "You must tell me seven moments in your life of the greatest significance. Only then will we know what good is in you."

"I told myself that it wasn't all that bad," the preacher sighed. "Boy, was I wrong." He lays his hands on his knees. "From the outside, it looked good. Except for the secret part that nobody knew about. One that carried, in my mind, no risk."

"What secret?" the Judge asks the preacher.

"We were having a fundraiser for the church and local charities. It took months of planning and many community members spent weeks preparing for this day. Oh, it was a glorious sunny day, everything I had asked God for the previous night."

"Along with other community members, I helped raise the tents, prepare the tables, and lay out the baked goods for sale. There were face-painting booths for the children, a Ferris wheel, jumping castles, a tea garden, and pie-eating contests all lined up for the day. That morning, I remember standing at the podium on stage with a smiling crowd of people waiting for me to open with a prayer to give blessings unto the day and welcome them."

"I said, 'Brothers and Sisters, on this fine morning, we come together not only to raise funds for those in need, but we also come together in the name of the Lord. It is with His blessing that we stand here today, healthy and ready to enjoy a day of laughter, hope, and love. Make this day yours and live it according to His will, as you should every day!'"

"The crowd clapped their hands. I could feel the rising pride in my chest. Yes, this was the reason I became a servant of God: to spread the word of God and relish in the hope and love of my community. I also knew that none of this would be possible if I hadn't made sacrifices of my own. But yet, I didn't regret one moment of it. Men and women, boys and girls, grandfathers and grandmothers, all were here to enjoy a day that I made possible."

"*You* made possible?" the Judge asks the preacher.

The preacher hesitates, "Well . . . yes."

"Well then, please continue," the Judge says.

Suddenly, the preacher man, who was filled with pride only a few moments ago, furrowed his brow and hung his head as he continued with his second story.

"I knew from the very beginning that I was setting myself up for a huge mistake. But I am only human after all, and even I sin at one point or another. It all began with Simon. There was something about him that I just couldn't explain. Yes, he was just a young kid, but he was funny and intelligent. He made me laugh, and his eyes sparkled whenever I talked to him. At first, I thought I just enjoyed his company, but then I developed strange feelings; feelings I couldn't explain. I prayed to God to take these feelings away, but no matter how hard I tried, I knew I just had to have Simon to myself."

"But what made the entire situation worse was the fact that I had the same feelings when talking to Harper, one of the young women living a block away from me. There was no denying it, I was attracted to her as well."

"It felt like I was living a double life. The things I preached against in church were the very things raging inside my own soul. It started to keep me up at night; I just couldn't forget about Simon's long, slender legs or Harper's seductive smile. No matter how hard I tried, there was no running from their faces. They kept haunting me. To help me forget, I went to a night club out of the city where I knew no one would recognize me. I needed to forget, and the only way I could do that was by having a few drinks."

"I had never even had a glass of wine before, and with one shot of tequila after the other filling me up, I knew I was stumbling down the wrong path. But I didn't care; as long as I could get away from the growing urge to meet with Simon or Harper."

"But one evening, I happened to drive past Harper's house. She was alone; I could see her sitting on the front porch with a glass of wine in her hand. She looked so beautiful, so young, so . . ." the preacher's voice trailed off.

He stood up and started pacing the room. "I couldn't stay away. It was as if she was a drug; something I simply had to have. I craved her; just like I craved Simon. At that very moment, I gave in to my willpower and approached her. I was not sure whether she thought I was drunk or the fact that she could be with a preacher without any strings attached, but she didn't deny me."

"When I returned home later that night, I cried and repented. I begged God to forgive me, yet I knew I would be back to see Harper. I also knew I had a new sense of confidence to approach Simon . . ."

* * *

James opens his car door and slumps himself into the driver's seat. He needs to get some fresh air and get away from set for a while. Suddenly, he gets an alert from his smartphone. Without thinking, he pulls it out and sees a new text message from Sage. James barely even glances up from his phone as he quickly texts back in reply. As he texts, he fails to notice that the traffic in front of him has stopped. Finally, he glances up . . .

He jams on the brakes, tires squealing . . . his eyes widen in disbelief. *Is this really happening*, he thinks as his perception of time slows to a crawl. Then, everything fades to black in James's mind, as the only sound to be heard is a resounding crash.

An overhead view of the crash scene. For James, his view begins to pull back, away from the scene, until the vehicles are nothing but small specks.

The clouds zoom past as he feels himself fly higher and higher. . . and the light of Heaven and its stars flare into a burst of pure white.

"The Lord loves everyone equally. Regardless of what they do with their talent, mind, and bodies," the Judge says.

"Oh, I loved Him too," the preacher says as he sits next to the Judge.

"You lived two lives: one of teaching the word of God from the pulpit and another of pursuing money and sex. You deceived the people who put their faith in you. You broke away from the love and the law of God."

"I did a lot of good for others." The chair across from him is now empty. He is momentarily bewildered.

The Judge stands by his side and places a hand on his shoulder. "I have made my decision."

"I'm sorry! Give me another chance," the preacher pleads.

"Follow me."

The Judge points to the two escalators—one going up and one going down. He looks at the preacher before firmly pointing to the down escalator.

The preacher mutely shakes his head. The Judge firmly takes his arm and leads him onto the descending escalator. The look of horror on the preacher's face is indescribable. A red light reflects upon him, emanating from somewhere down below. The man opens his mouth as if to say something, but then he sinks out of sight.

The Judge stands in front of the escalator with his hands folded behind his back. He looks down into the depths and pauses for a moment before returning back to his chair in the booth. He looks at the empty chair across from him while shaking his head.

"Blessed are those who even with a broken heart refrain from the actions of false servants of God. They don't let their soul be damaged but keep the faith and love for our Lord."

* * *

James tries to recollect where he was. All he can remember is that he was in a car crash. He places his hands on the glassy floor, thinking that it will crack, but it doesn't. He quickly turns his eyes from the floor upwards to notice there is no roof over his head, only sky and clouds above. He hears a voice in the distance. He squints his eyes as he tries to eavesdrop on what sounds like a serious discussion. However, the more he tries to listen, the fainter the voices become.

His surroundings feel surreal; the glossy floor gives the space a soft feeling. Not only does James feel lighter, but from his reflection on the ground, he appears younger in age. He is confused by his youthful appearance and his strange surroundings, and though he does not scorn the image of his younger self, he cannot bother about it now. He looks up to see if the voices are coming from the nearby speakers, but he is disappointed to hear them disappear again. The sky is radiant in shades of blue like those old times when he counted the hopeful stars as a teenager.

As he moves forward, he notices two escalators in the far corner. They look menacing. He sees a woman in her thirties sitting and talking on a telephone as if she is a secretary behind a large desk made of mother-of-pearl. Two tall men standing in crisp white suits and wearing dark sunglasses behind her. They have gossamer wings that don't appear capable of lifting the muscular men. The men momentarily distract him from the angelic woman. Her voice is sharp and her tone firm; her small eyes remind James of the Sharapova event. He had a lover there . . . but this is not time to think about that.

"Yes, sir. We're almost at maximum." She pauses before adding, "Very well. I understand."

As James walks towards her, he notices a few other items on her desk, including a rubber stamp and a very long list. The woman hangs up the phone and looks up at him expectantly.

"Hello. My name is Fate. We've been expecting you," says the woman in white.

"Is that Faith, like, believing?"

"No, Fate . . . as in destiny."

"You have wings," says James cautiously.

"Yes. Most of us do around here," Fate confirms.

He pauses, craning his neck to take a quick peek at his back. Nope. No wings there. If he lifted his shirt, his back probably still has the scar he has had since he was a child.

Fate notices his motion and says, "You have to earn them."

He raises his eyebrows as he glances back at a smiling Fate, "Where am I?"

"At my desk. Hand, please." Fate reaches her hand out towards James, turning her palm up to accept his.

James stands silently.

"Your hand, please."

After a moment, he slowly extends his right hand and Fate abruptly stamps it. Surprised, he pulls his hand back and stares at the stamp that reads the number thirty on it in blue ink. "What is this?" asks James.

"Haven't you been to a club before?"

He looks around, "Sure, but never one like this."

"The show is about to start. Certainly, don't want to be late."

He tries to protest, "But I don't understand. What is . . ."

Fate interrupts him. "Go on, Mr. Glass. Your time has come."

"Time for what? Where am I going?"

"To the thirtieth floor. It's right there on your hand." She says this like it's the most obvious thing in the world. "Follow the hall down and take the escalator up."

"The escalator? I thought it was supposed to be a stairway," he says, thinking out loud.

"It used to be," Fate says while smiling. "We've modernized."

He studies her face, but it betrays nothing. Her face is riddled with little smiles. With just a glance, he could see her excitement. *But why would she not be excited to elucidate 'newcomers'?* James thinks. *Seems like a fun job.*

"One last bit of advice, Mr. Glass." Fate says gesturing towards the escalator hallway, "Keep focused upon your destination and on what lies ahead. The escalator will automatically stop on your floor."

He holds up his hand and stares at the number thirty stamped on it. He nods and begins to walk away before turning back for another look at Fate.

She is already speaking to a new arrival. A Chinese woman steps up to the desk. Fate gives the woman a warm smile and without missing a beat she transitions her language to communicate with the woman. Their discussion fades away as James cautiously approaches the escalator, not knowing what awaits him along the way.

An effeminate French man is next in line at Fate's desk; she stamps his hand. Fate begins to speak French to him.

"Bonjour. J'me appel Fate. Nous vous attendions. NumÈro 29 porte. Prendre l'escalator."

The French man nods and says, "Merci."

There is another man standing behind him in line. As he steps away from Fate's desk, the man behind him breaks out into an intolerant attack, calling out, "His kind will go directly to Hell! The Bible has Adam and Eve, not Adam and Steve!" Do they call you 'Petra'?"

The French man hears and quickly turns, yelling in French towards the angry man who wears a patch over one of his eyes.

Crying and out of breath, the man screams back, "What did you say to me?" The man spits as he tries to grabs the French man by the arms, but he begins to walk backward.

Suddenly, the angel bouncers appear and quickly intervene. Fate gestures to the angry man, her eyes dangerously flashing, a fierce look for someone so outwardly gentle. Her eyes reflect the bright light of her surroundings as if they were mirrors in the sun. She shines the light from her eyes to scare the men into complacency.

"Enough!" Fate says firmly. "Your hatred and poison words are not welcome here. You humans think yourselves worthy to judge your fellow man without considering your own flaws. However, you are no longer on Earth, and you will no longer judge another being again. You will be judged by Him."

One of the bulky guards leads the one-eyed man back to his place in line as the French man proceeds down the hallway to find his escalator. Fate says, "Proceed with your journey."

James is riding upward; he is no longer alone.

33

"How did you get up here so fast?" James asks.

"It was Fate who sent you up here," says the familiar-looking woman.

"Aren't you Fate?"

"Fate?" the woman says, amused.

"You know, Fate, as in destiny?"

"No, I am Faith. As in belief," she says smiling.

"Are you twin sisters?"

Faith nods, "Yes, except for the wings. We are unique, as are all souls."

Then James notices many large video screens set flush into the walls alongside the escalator, similar to those in large, modern airports.

"It's better if you don't look," Faith tells him.

"Then, why are they even here?"

"Faith asks, 'why is there temptation?'"

As he reaches the first screen, he is fascinated by the strange imagery displayed upon it.

On the first screen, James sees a man, about thirty-three years old, screaming. He is strapped to a table with a buzz-saw pointing directly at his groin. His scream is so loud that James has to block his ear holes to muffle the horrid sound.

James glances at Faith, "What is this?"

"I believe some people call it . . . justice," she says gently.

He glances back at the screen to see the blade getting closer to shredding the man in half. James closes his eyes and says, "If this is justice as you say, then surely this man must have done evil on earth."

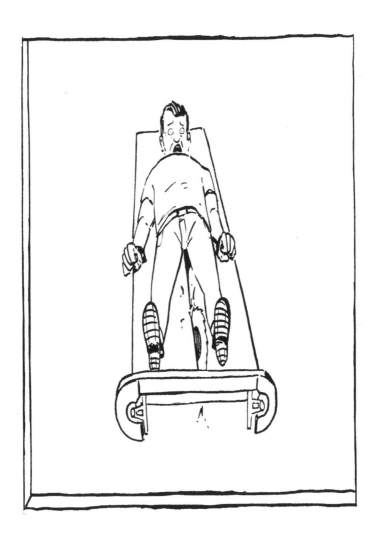

"He was a child molester, and that is how he will spend his eternity," Faith curtly states. James is surprised to hear the man's crime. He did not look like a criminal. James looks away quickly, but his thoughts are his own as the man attempts to scream his way to freedom.

As the escalator continues to rise, the next screen captures James's attention. He considers not giving in to the temptation again, but he figures: *Can't be worse than the last one . . .*

A man also about thirty-three years old struggles to walk on the pavement. He is bent forward by the weight of assault rifles strewn across his back, and he also tows a cart full of guns behind him. Bandoliers of ammunition crisscross his chest and pistols are holstered at his belt. Even before James asks the question, he perceives that the man must have been a murderer. The man's grizzled face appears to be somewhat familiar as if James has seen him once on television.

"Why?" James asks, distracted by the grumbling cry of the man as he slides past.

"One of the monsters you call an 'active shooter.' He used those guns to murder dozens of innocent people. And I am not showing you what happens to him next..." James think, *"if we don't have sensible gun laws, the unending race for more and bigger guns will bring more killers here and more massacre down there..."*

Then a third screen calls to him. This screen is larger than the past two screens, held in place by two giant pillars. For an idle moment, James wonders if the screens are categorized into the level of atrocities committed.

A woman who also appears to be in her early thirties stands in front of a stop sign. As moments pass, James realizes she does not move and seems confused. He wonders why she is frozen in place.

"Why is that woman just stopped there?"

"That is all she will ever do," Faith confirms.

"What do you mean?" James says with confused concern.

"She was an alcoholic. She swore to stop drinking and could not keep the promise she made to herself. One night while driving drunk she badly injured half a dozen people, all of whom managed to escape alive, luckily. Her punishment is the eternal reminder that she should have stopped when she had the chance."

James finds it difficult to understand how the eternal punishments correspond with each error committed by the people on the screens. He also tries to comprehend why their suffering is put on display.

In his curious state, James's eyes search the images on the next screen. It is a young couple, about thirty-three years old sitting on a bench kissing and hugging one another.

"They've been married for sixty years, and both chose each other in the end." Faith smiles. "Very romantic, no?"

"Wait. What do you mean they chose each other?" James quickly retorts.

"Each was judged. Each was given a choice. It so happens that their choices were mutual," Faith says as she presses her hands together to demonstrate, "completion of the union."

"But sixty years? They look like a young couple, honeymooners maybe."

"Yes. They are thirty-three years old to be exact."

He turns away from the screen to look at Faith. "Why?"

"You begin to truly live your life at thirty-three; Jesus died at thirty-three; three days passed from His death to His glorious resurrection; The Holy Trinity; the Three Kings . . . I can go on . . ."

"And the Three Musketeers, the Three Stooges . . ." James giggles behind a childish smirk. Realizing that Faith isn't amused, he quickly returns to his serious composure before saying, "Actually, I remember reading somewhere that the number three signifies divine perfection."

"Life isn't about perfection. It's about choices and how they mark the makeup of the person," Faith says.

James begins to contemplate his own life and his decisions, from his first girlfriend to his marriage, he recalls how his choices have impacted the mindset that has set him apart to this day.

James then notices a large group of people approaching the young couple on screen looking as if they are inviting them to a game of baseball.

"Who are they?" James asks.

Faith looks at the screen and smiles warmly, "They are the moms, dads, grandparents, the entirety of the family who all lived in love of God. They are all together in Heaven now."

"Heaven?" James says, shifting his eyes around this strange place where he has found himself.

"Is this Heaven?"

Faith remains silent and looks upwards at the escalator.

"How many screens are there?" James asks.

"More than you could ever imagine."

"The escalator isn't that long."

Faith smiles, "It is far longer than you can comprehend."

James considers her statement then slowly turns to examine the next screen. He notices that the screen sits upon the base of a rocket as if about to be launched into space. It has a four-dimensional effect, and its booming sound feels as if it is hitting him directly in the face.

Faith gives him a sideways glance, then holds up her hand, "Allow me to show you something else."

Suddenly, the screen clicks on to show a room that resembles some sort of country club waiting room with a recreational area, so vast it even boasts practice golf courses. James blinks in confusion. He knows for certain that he has seen this place before, as if it were déjà vu, but he cannot decipher if it is another set of moving images, a dream, or something conjured from his head.

James notices that there are several young-looking people gathered around the place; some are reading, others playing billiards or card games. Occasionally they glance at the bank of clocks hanging along the back wall.

"Are they waiting for something?" James asks.

Faith responds, "Indeed, they are waiting for the ones they love, the ones they chose to be with, and hoping that they will be chosen in the same manner."

"That doesn't seem like a very peaceful eternity . . . waiting around for someone to show up and maybe select you back," James says curtly.

"That's one way to look at it," Faith says before extending her arm towards a wide hallway. "We have arrived."

As James and Faith step off the escalator, James sees the entrance to what looks like the outside of a classic disco club. They walk up to red velvet ropes and Faith lifts the hook off the stanchion, guiding James inside and toward the DJ booth in the back corner.

She motions for him to take a seat then suddenly disappears without a sound.

James scans the room and the DJ equipment surrounding him. Bewildered, he takes a heavy breath and sinks into the chair. When he opens his eyes with a sigh, there is a man standing beside him, and he kicks back in his seat with surprise. James can sense that the man is highly important, some sort of authority, definitely powerful. The man sits in front of James.

"Welcome, James."

This is a man unlike anyone James has ever seen before in his life. His presence in the room practically glows and looms large. He does not have wings but floats around the room as if he gliding on water. There weren't any pearly gates to be seen, but surely this man was the Judge himself?

"Where am I?" James asks with desperation.

A cell phone begins to ring, and the man pulls it from what seems like thin air and guides it to his ear, "Yes, Fate?" There is a long pause before he says, "Open floors thirty-one and thirty-two."

As James receives the attention of the man, he feels disoriented as he begins to recall some unusual thoughts, possibly memories.

"The last thing I remember, I was driving my car ..." James begins to say before his voice trails off.

"I've never driven a car. We don't need them around here," says the man, "some people find joy in the freedom of driving, but I find my joy through music. Do you like music, James?"

James continues to sit silently stunned by the clash of his memories and the confusing situation at hand and thinks, "I love music." He tries to recall the last song he heard. He even remembers once getting into an argument with a police officer about the appropriate decibel level for his radio while driving. *But I was a teenager back then . . . It's like time has no meaning here,* James thinks.

The man closes his eyes, "I daydream of driving a convertible down country roads listening to my favorite songs with the wind in my hair."

"Who are you?" James says, almost pleading.

"I have seen so many who thought nothing of driving while talking on a phone, putting on makeup, filling out a Sudoku puzzle, even procreating, if you can imagine. It is a strange thing," the man continues, "how human beings take the gift of life, created by God, so lightly. Shooting rampages, suicide, mass killings, not to mention laws put in place to justify these and many other tragedies without resolution."

James sits looking sober and calm, but his mind drifts, visualizing images of stories that did not belong to him.

James sees a teenage girl waiting outside an abortion clinic, her insensitive boyfriend waiting in his car, playing on his phone. She is ashamed and frightened but proceeds with her decision.

James sees a large crowd shouting and running for their lives in fear as they run away from the sound of gunshots in the background.

"I almost cannot keep up," the man continues. Suddenly, the man is behind him with his hands on the back of the chair.

"Who are you? What am I doing here?" James pleads again.

"I am the Judge. You are here to tell me the stories of your life."

"Stories of my life?" James repeats. "Am I dead?"

The Judge paces as he talks, gesturing with his hands and his expressive face. James wonders if this man is playing with his mind. James wonders if he is really dead.

"You are a movie man. You know how to tell stories or teach valuable lessons in a good parable. Most movies promote everything that people should not do, at least not if they want to enter the Kingdom of God. The audience dreams of becoming a fictional character or a larger-than-life superhero rather than live their lives in meaningful ways. Humans sometimes do not realize the aspects that they admire of these characters and miss the fact that they are acting in the ways of the real superhero, the Lord himself."

James shifts in his seat.

The Judge continues, "Now I ask that you tell me the most important stories of your life, James. The ones you have lived that have come to define you as the person you are today."

"I'm not sure I understand," says James looking concerned.

The Judge smiles as he looks at another screen then back to James, "Tell me about how you used your talents, loved and gave to others, and acted in accordance with God's will."

James looks down into his lap, contemplating, nervously wringing his hands.

"Seven to be exact, and then I will make my decision." The judge shows seven fingers.

"Decision?" James quickly remembers the man from the first screen with the wood saw at his groin. He remembers the woman standing alone at the stop sign waiting for nothing or something. He silently begins to reflect on his life and the pain sets in. His heart feels as if it is breaking. He sees it all now; his wrongs, his mistakes, and his regrets.

The Judge then appears sitting in the chair next to James and puts his hand on top of his hand to ease his concerns. "Tell me seven stories and then I will examine and judge your life," he says.

"My life . . ." James speaks to himself in a hushed voice.

"Depending on how you lived your life, either I will choose your eternity or you will. If you lived the majority of your life with esteem and goodness, then you shall pick who will accompany you in Heaven. If you lived the majority of your life acting wrongly and being wicked, then I will choose your fate.

James remembers the agonizing scream of the man under the saw, crying out in vain to deaf ears. He wonders who was the one controlling the saw anyway. *Could it be the Judge? Was God himself?*

The Judge walks over to a large wall of draperies and pulls the curtains aside to reveal a multimedia room behind it. The room's most eye-catching feature is a huge screen occupying the entire wall. On the screen is an image of an enormous sky, clouds drifting lazily past. The Judge walks to the huge screen and begins to manipulate it with his hands. The image shifts to that of the planet Earth from outer space. The familiar and delicate blue and green marble floating in total darkness. As the Judge manipulates the screen, he says, "This is our Heavenly station. From here I can see anyone and anything at any time, past or present."

The image of Earth grows closer and closer, zooming in quickly. The continents take shape, then the countries, then the cities, until finally the image draws tight to a view of city streets. The Judge did not select this place at random; he focuses on the United States, then on to the distinct shape of California, then to the City of Los Angeles, to the exact street where James had his car accident, the last thing he remembers.

James considers that this must be how the Judge knows so much about everything. *But where was God?* He thinks that he has lived a quite concise life and he did not have a riotous lifestyle, so perhaps he will be okay. But the screen makes him uneasy. *Has everything really been recorded?* He knows he has to tell the truth.

On the screen, the Judge zooms directly onto a smoking car and to the bystanders pulling a man's broken and bloody body from the wreckage.

The mortally injured James depicted on the screen stares wide-eyed upwards into the sky as the Judge and James stare down at him.

James jerks back as if burned, almost falling backward. The image before him shakes him to the core. He begins to hyperventilate. He is shocked to see that this is how he finally dies. He examines his body from this great distance by way of the giant screen.

The Judge gives James a sideways glance, then slides a hand across the screen before it goes dark. In the mirror-like glass, James sees his reflection and realizes that he, too, is thirty-three years old again. In a daze, he stumbles back toward the chair. "This isn't a dream. I really am dead."

James cradles his head in his hands. The Judge briefly lays a hand on his shoulder, "Death is not the end, James. It is more like the middle. It is the nature of things to come in stages. God created the world that way too. Death is merely a transition between life and afterlife."

He thinks for a moment then asks, "So what comes next?"

"Begin to visualize your story. Bring it to life for me in such a way that I will also visualize it. It should be easy for you," says the Judge.

"Because I'm a director?"

"Because you are an excellent storyteller. There is nothing more wonderful than the theater of the mind."

He is reminded of meditation classes where everything is centered on the clarity of the mind and understands the request.

James nervously adjusts in his chair, frantically thinking of a million days at once. He glances over at the Heavenly Judge and uses his forearm to wipe the sweat beading on his forehead. He closes his eyes and opens his mouth to speak when suddenly the lights in the disco start to glow and the colors shimmer and flare across the walls. The

Judge magically cues up some music that changes based on James's tone as if it were the living soundtrack to a movie.

"Here goes . . ."

* * *

"It's 1995, and I am twenty-two years old and the shining star of film school." James laughs. He sees a much younger version of himself, complete with his trusty red baseball cap and VHS movie camera. He is standing on the rooftop of a building on his college campus. He still goes by the childhood nickname, "Jimbo."

"Come on! Jump!" James yells to his friend and fellow student, Rick.

Rick is dressed in a Superman costume complete with a cape that waves as he jumps off the building into the air. His fantastic flight is quickly cut short by gravity as he lands on a battered mattress they hauled up to a lower roof.

"That looked great, bro!" James grins and gives a thumbs-up. "Let's wrap this. If security catches us filming up here again without permission, he's going to tear us apart."

"Dude, he's not even a real cop. He just acts like one," Rick says. "So, he can only fake arrest us."

"Well, he's got a nightstick, and he especially hates you like a cold toilet seat!" James gives a dismissive wave and readies for another take.

"Are you kidding me? Are . . . you . . . kidding . . . me!" Security Specialist Sergeant Collie shouts from the stairwell door. Rick and James whip their heads around to see the campus security officer as he raises a whistle to his lips. "Stop! Or I'll tear you both apart," he yells as he begins to run towards them.

"Don't you mean stop or I'll say stop again?" Rick shouts, mockingly. James grabs his camera and tripod and begins running towards the second stairwell. Rick quickly follows behind as his superhero cape whips back in the wind.

The security guard continues to blow his whistle as he follows James and Rick to the ground floor. They run across the wide field to the Art and Science Library and slow their pace as they approach the entrance, where another security guard is standing watch. As they enter the building, James suggests they should, "Split up." They part ways inside.

Rick ducks behind the towering stacks, using the book-cases for cover. James spots an empty chair across from someone reading a newspaper. He immediately slips into the vacant seat. The woman across from him wears a hoodie and holds the paper very close to her face.

The newspaper lowers, and there sits the twenty-year-old Kate, in her college days. She was beautiful and smart, and James could never quite summon up the courage to speak to her. One, because she was a "freshman" and two, he didn't want anything serious while doing his "productions." That is, until now. "Excuse me, can I borrow the sports section?" James asks.

She raises an eyebrow, then slowly tosses the sports sections across the table. He flips up the paper to hide his face just as the security guard hurries past.

Kate lowers her paper again. "Are you on the lam or something?" she asks.

"As a matter of fact, I am," James replies.

"Uh, you're not exactly running from the FBI there, Mr. Dillinger . . . But I'd still like to know why I'm harboring a fugitive."

James slips the camera out of his backpack to show her. "Finishing my first film. I'm going to be a famous director one day. Win a bunch of awards . . ."

"Wow. Law-abiding and humble." Her sarcasm makes James smile. He loves how she twists her hands when she calls him humble. Her fingers spiral as she drops the newspaper with the other hand.

"What's your major? Besides sarcasm."

Kate laughs, then replies, "Art."

"Cool. Does that mean you want to draw me naked?"

"I'm a painter."

"Cool, you want to paint me naked?" James asked slyly.

"Not really, no." She looks to the side before saying, "Your friend is back."

James looks up and sees that she's right. Collie is making his way toward them, using his nightstick to push down newspapers to better see the faces hiding behind them.

"Got to go. It's been a pleasure."

He un-asses the seat and heads for the stairs. The security guard sees him and takes off in hot pursuit!

James runs up the stairs, going hard. He can hear the sounds of Collie pursuing him. The out-of-shape security guard sputters and gasps for air. The security guard knows he can't catch James and starts blowing his whistle to call for assistance.

James emerges from the stairs onto the roof. He looks for an escape route . . . The roof of the next building is only about three feet away. *I can probably make that,* James thinks. *Probably.*

Collie finally arrives on the roof, wheezing loudly from the exertion, but still in dogged pursuit. With no other choice, James hefts his camera and runs full speed toward the ledge . . .

Down below, Kate has emerged from the Library and is watching the whole thing from ground level.

James jumps the divide between the buildings. But something falls free during the leap! Between the terror of running for his life and not falling to his death, James doesn't notice. . . .

James comes to a rolling landing on the next roof and keeps going. Collie can't make the jump and continues to blast his whistle ineffectually. Kate walks over to see what James had dropped. James's film reel lays on the ground. Kate jumps of pleasure, at discovering this unexpected souvenir of her interaction with James, then carefully picks it up off the ground.

* * *

The Judge arches an eyebrow while gesturing James to stop telling the story.

"James, James . . . You do understand what's going on here? You are fighting for your afterlife. These tales will decide your destiny. Why are you telling me such a little story?"

Feeling a little annoyed, James says, "You need to be patient, uh, Your Honor. I like to develop my stories. So, sit tight and listen. There's a lot of subtext going on here. Jeez, everybody's a critic."

James glances at the Judge, "May I continue?"

The Judge waves a hand as if to say, "Go ahead."

* * *

The next day, James was really upset. He couldn't even go to math class. Which he usually skipped anyways because it was at 8 a.m. But you have to understand that he felt the pain of his lost tape and that all the work was gone. These were the days before digital, so everything was on that film reel . . .

James is sitting on a bench, head down. There are sunflowers growing behind it. The sun making an easy heat on his skin as he tries to think himself through his current predicament. He has his notebook with him and scribbles a few notes; at first, they appear incomprehensible but later it becomes obvious he is trying to make a calendar for a new film shoot.

"You look like you lost your best friend." Kate pulls the film reel out of her bag and dangles it in front of him.

Seeing the film reel, he lights up and reaches for it, but Kate snatches it back. She thinks his desperation makes him look more interesting. He quickly puts his notepad aside as he makes a deliberate move this time to reach out for the reel. "Hey, that's mine!" he protests to Kate.

Slender and sexy, Kate uses her height to keep the film reel just out of James's reach. "You're a director, right? So, you have a good eye?"

"Sure," James replies.

"I have my first art exhibition coming up, and I need someone to film it and also take a couple still photos of my work for the promotional flyer."

James considers this for a moment, eyeing his lost footage. "Okay, you got a deal." James quickly realizes that this is a golden opportunity to spend more time around Kate. *Wow* . . . James finally felt lucky for the first time in his entire life. This beautiful freshman girl he couldn't summon up the nerve to talk to is in the right place at the right time to save him from Collie, find his lost film reel, and now she's blackmailing him with it to hang out with her? Had he been a lesser "macho man," he probably would have fallen to his knees to thank God right then and there.

Kate sits down beside him and hands the film to him. She suddenly leans right into his personal space, grabs James face with both hands, and starts kissing him passionately. James's eyes open in wide shock, but quickly begin to close slowly as he relaxes and enjoys the kiss.

Collie barely gives them a second glance as he passes by. "Get a room," he scoffs.

Kate abruptly breaks off the kiss, letting James up for air. He is very surprised to see Collie departing and then he realizes . . .

"Wow. That's twice you've saved my ass." Kate has won his heart after this wonderful move.

Leaning so close to her, James notices a necklace with a gold nameplate charm dangling just above her cleavage: KATE.

He can only imagine what it would be like kissing down from her neck, across her nameplate, down to her cleavage . . .

He snaps off a sunflower from behind the bench and hands it to her. "Thanks . . . Kate." He has never been able to express love like this before. He had been in love once or twice, but it seemed meeting with Kate was just so perfect.

Kate takes the flower with a smile and hoists her backpack over her shoulder. "Meet me back here around five o'clock with your equipment, okay? I'll take you over to the Art Museum." She pauses, "Hey, you didn't tell me your name."

"I'm James, but everybody just calls me Jimbo."

Kate starts walking backward. "Okay, James. I'll see you tonight."

"Hey . . . Everybody calls me Jimbo."

Kate shakes her head while saying, "I'm not everybody."

* * *

James snaps back to reality and feels himself grinning at the scene of his younger self. "The moment I met Kate, I realized I could spend the rest of my life with her. She was daring and passionate. In my mind, I saw us with four children and producing a lifetime movie, and I loved making movies back then. Things weren't so complicated."

"You sound envious of those days," the Heavenly Judge says.

"Sometimes I am. Life can be hard."

The Judge is gone again. James scans the disco and locates the Judge standing on the dance floor. He walks over to join him.

"You think death is easy?" he asks.

"I don't know yet."

"You sound annoyed."

"I guess I don't like the idea of having to defend myself. And the choices I made."

"I cannot recall saying that you had to . . . More often than not, the decisions we make speak for themselves."

James opens his mouth to answer but decides to not say anything at all. Since the start of this meeting with the Judge, he had been defending himself. He decided it was better if he just kept silent and watched how things played out.

"One last question before we move on," says the Judge.

"Sure."

The Judge's eyes glitter in the light as they bore into James's soul while asking, "Who do you want to spend eternity with?"

James had so many experiences left he would love to share, and he did not actually care for the way the "last question" sounded coming from the Judge. But he knew he could live with anything as long as he was not sentenced to carrying a heavy load all throughout eternity.

James does not make eye contact with the Judge, all the while he has tried to do so, yet he has been unable. Hence whenever he looks up, it looks just like the Judge has gone out of his presence again. All the time, he tries to relate the story to him, and at the same time, he is looking to see if the Judge is still around.

He looks up and realizes the Judge is gone yet again and he is alone on the dance floor. The Judge is back in his chair at the booth. James returns to the DJ Booth and takes a seat, remaining silent.

The Judge starts his next music track. "There we go. Tell me another story."

James likes the current song that the Judge has chosen. He realizes he used the same track for one of his short films in school. "Nice. I would have totally let you score one of my films," James mentions.

This makes the Judge laugh.

James begins his story to the Judge. He knows that this story will do a lot in determining his destiny; and from time to time, his mind flashes back to those persons he saw screaming for help as he entered this place.

* * *

"Less than six months later, we were engaged." James laughs as he continues his story, "Then graduating and getting married and before we knew it Kate was. . ."

James's voice trails off as he visualizes his memory. He is in a nice field with low, mowed grass and a picnic area with tables and gazebos nearby. Kate is wearing a sundress and looks a little older but still beautiful, lying on her side on a blanket, getting some sun. Her pregnant belly shows the sign of a new life growing at a rapid pace and gives James joy because it is his first child.

She smiles and rubs her stomach, feeling the baby kick. The wedding band on her finger catches the sunlight and flickers with an invisible promise. She holds a sunflower in her hand, lowers her sunglasses, and smiles over at Rick and James taking shots of the area with movie cameras in hand.

James's finger is also adorned with a simple wedding band, and when he gestures toward a nearby wooded area, Kate shakes her head. She then grimaces in pain, her hand going back to her swollen abdomen.

Kate was always a very strong woman; she seemed to have her life planned out with every detail and precise action. She visits her doctor regularly to be certain of her expected delivery date. *She is very unlike me,* James thinks, knowing for certain that if that baby were in his belly instead, they would only have found out the due date when the labor started!

"That looks really good for the woodland sequences. Come on, let's roll some footage for an establishing shot," James tells Rick.

"Dude, these look like the same damned woods you said didn't work ten minutes ago," Rick responds.

James laughs as he says, "Who are you, Forest Ranger Rick? You can identify trees by sight now?"

Rick grins as he joins in on the joke, "Yeah, I'm like a friggin' squirrel. You want to hold my nuts for me?"

A piercing scream quickly ends their conversation. They both snap their heads around to see Kate sitting up on the blanket, both hands curved around her belly.-

"She's coming!" Kate exclaims.

Rick and James exchange a confused look, checking the forest around them.

"The baby, you idiots!" Kate confirms.

They start hauling ass to get to Kate. Their male instincts had made them both not understand her initial scream. James says, "Dude, I thought she meant some crazy witch was emerging from the woods!" What else would be expected from some confused fellows who had just been rolling cameras all their college days?

Rick tries making another joke, "Nope, she's already here."

While James gives him a stern look, Rick grins and shrugs.

"Hurry up! Ohmigod, ohmigod. It hurts so bad! We got to go! Run faster!"

James helps Kate into the car, as Rick jumps behind the wheel.

"You're not driving my car!" James yells.

"Shut up, you drive slower than my granny. And she's dead," Rick announces and winks at Kate. He and Kate always laugh at the way James's driving was so painfully slow.

James jumps in the car beside his wife.

"Punch it!" Kate screams.

Rick stands on the gas pedal and the car fishtails into gear. James's convertible roars down the small rural highway, which is luckily pretty devoid of traffic. James got the car from an award he had won shooting a picture. He had over time taunted Rick about the car; hence, he was reluctant for Rick to be behind the wheel.

James squeezes his wife's hand. She's trying to control her breathing and is sweating profusely. Her eyes roll back and forth, her body shifting trying to get comfortable.

Kate tries talking in between breaths, "How . . . far . . . to . . . the hospital?"

"We got at least ten miles," Rick says.

Kate looks over at James and whispers, "She's not going to wait that long."

"Are you serious?" James exclaims.

"Do I look like I'm kidding!"

James pats Rick's arm, "Pull over."

"What?" the message gets through to Rick, but he hears the opposite. He hits the pedal harder and the car goes flying faster than before.

"Do it!" James says while pointing. "There is a mile marker over there. Go there, so we have a reference. And give me your phone."

Rick reaches over his shoulder and hands him an old school nineties brick phone.

"I only have seventy-five minutes this month, talk fast."

James punches in the number 911 on the display. Rick absently wonders if James is trying to bring help this way or just trying to get a guide through the delivery process.

When he hears someone answer on the other side, James speaks, "Yes, I have an emergency. My wife is pregnant." He did not even know what to say, but he felt mentioning the fact that his wife was pregnant would trigger the level of alertness he needed.

He then has a pause before he adds, "She's about to give birth! Like now! Listen, we just left Pines Park, and we're on the way to East Regional Hospital."

"We're not going to make it!" Kate yells again. He tries to think of a way to convey the urgency of Kate's situation to the person on the other side of the phone, but then again, he feels using her own words would be just fine.

He quickly adds, "But I don't think we're going to make it. Send us some help! Please!"

James listens to the instructions given to him from the other end of the phone and confirms, "Okay, we're pulling over now. Hold on, we're at Mile Marker 249." He says this as he places one of his hands, on Kate's. He knows he has to keep holding her hand until she is finally attended to. He can feel her breath, and anytime it seems that he can no longer hear her, he quickly squeezes her palm to get her attention.

Kate leans back, holding her stomach as if trying to keep the baby in. "Hold on, hold on, little girl. Not yet," she whispers.

As they pull over to the side of the road, he hands the brick phone back to Rick. "The ambulance is on the way. Just hang in there, Kate." He tries to calm her nerves and make her more comfortable.

While shaking her head, Kate says, "I can't. She's coming. No . . . Oooooowwwwwwww!" She starts pivoting in pain on the back seat to sit sideways across it. This is a mark of fear for James. She is obviously not going to be able to hold on for long. She was going to deliver that baby all by herself.

James climbs out to give her some room, leaving the door open and crouching in the space there. He makes sure she has enough space to deliver the baby herself.

Rick looks back, eyes wide. "Oh my God, this is really happening." Rick has been very much silent since the whole drama began.

James nods while saying, "Get the camera ready." James feels he needs to capture this moment perfectly just so he can reference it later in the future. He knows it is important to record something neither he nor Kate would want to miss.

Rick readies the camera, peering through. He adjusts the contrast to achieve a clear, perfect view.

As he sees Kate's facial expression, he says, "Kate, did you forget to wear makeup today? You look a little shiny in frame . . ."

"I swear to God I'm going to shove that camera right up your ass. And around the corner," Kate hisses.

In the back seat of the car, Kate lets out a scream and snarls at Rick again, who is getting in front of her. She lifts her knees and spreads her legs, the sun-dress riding up her thighs. Rick has climbed out of the car to get a perfect view of the delivery. He places the camera just in front of Kate while she is laying in the back seat with her legs open; it is the best spot to get his eyes on the process.

"She's coming now. Do you see her?" Kate asks.

Although reluctant, James starts looking for what might be the baby's head. "Yesssss."

Kate groans loudly while Rick continues filming. The initial plan James had with Kate was that he would make the film while the nurses attended to her but where they found themselves currently made James unprofessionally busy; although he did not have the expertise to know what to do, his undivided attention was needed especially by Kate.

"So, have you guys picked out a name yet?" Rick asks.

"Lynn," Kate says. At the same time that James says, "Jenna." Even at this crucial time, James would not even exchange his usual bantering with Kate. He takes a quick glance at Kate immediately as he says a different name; her face is a mixture of glow and anguish.

"Uh, which is it?" Rick looks confused.

Kate and James engage in a quick stare-down contest, spaghetti western style.

"Honey, we agreed that we'd name her after my grand-mother," Kate explains.

"No, I'm pretty sure we agreed we'd name her after my grandmother," James says.

Kate groans as she's hit with another contraction. If she had not had this distraction, James would not have a chance in this argument.

"Crap! I missed that. Could you do that one more time?" Rick says, holding the camera.

"What! Is he kidding?" Clearly pissed, Kate snarls at Rick, "This is childbirth, you idiot! You don't get any re-takes!" Rick puts up a short smile in response to Kate's comment, he knew what and how exactly to get Kate pissed, and he just did. Of course, he would never have gotten away with this if Kate was not in delivery.

James had been there all through the process, trying very hard to give Kate the best response she could get in situations like this. He would look at Kate and once in a while peep through the dashboard to see if the ambulance was arriving.

She looks at James while saying through gritted teeth, "James, she's coming out. I need you to get down there and introduce yourself to our daughter." James looks strange, as he bends his head into Kate's lap. He needs to get a perfect look to see what Kate is talking about. He says something not very clear then quickly moves his head out of her lap and tells her she will be okay.

Reluctantly, he nods. "I'm really sorry about all this, Kate."

"Honey, you don't have to be sorry. It's a very pretty spot, don't you think? I mean, no doctors or nurses or sick people or that awful hospital smell."

"I have to tell you, babe, right now I wouldn't mind a doctor being here."

"We did something together no one else could . . . We made her."

"You mean Jenna? Push," James says.

"No, I mean Lynn. Nice try," Kate catches his joke.

They share a smile, and James suddenly has a great idea. "Hey! What about Jenna Lynn?"

"Okay, I like that," Kate agrees.

Kate then lets out a bloodcurdling scream.

James's eyes widen as he screams too, "Here she comes! One more push!"

Suddenly, James sees a baby, and the sound of a new-born cry fills the air. "She's beautiful." Rick stands there speechless. He is shocked that he has just made history with James and his family. It is a very good feeling as he continues to film; he makes sure to capture everything, up to the road where they were. He takes the camera to the front of the car, getting a perfect view of Kate in the car from that angle; he just wants to get everything.

James can only imagine the journeys he will share with his daughter:

Kate and James take turns pacing the floor with baby Jenna Lynn at midnight trying to calm her down and get her to sleep. Kate and James along with young Jenna Lynn at the beach, collecting seashells and building a sandcastle.

James teaching a young Jenna Lynn to play the piano. They sit together on the piano bench, and he guides her fingers over the keys . . . singing together. At her easel nearby, Kate watches in amusement as she paints a beautiful sunny sky and then joins in . . .

Kate and James getting Jenna Lynn ready for her first day of school, adjusting her backpack. She waves goodbye as she runs out the door to catch the bus, leaving her parents behind with tears in their eyes.

James abruptly wipes a tear from his eyes with the back of his hand as he comes back to reality. Kate smiles and then leans her head back on the seat, utterly exhausted from the delivery. He hears sirens in the background, getting closer . . .

* * *

Realizing that he is sitting in the disco booth, James wipes a tear from his eyes. He leans back in the chair and looks over to where the Judge is listening to his story.

"Nothing changes your life as much as creating a new one," James says.

"I find it difficult to believe that someone can watch a child being born and not believe there is a God," the Judge muses.

"Yet some people don't. That has to be hard, you know . . . for Him."

"No different than any other parent who watches his child turn away from them."

"Kate and I really made a good team back then."

"A good marriage is a blessing."

James looked at the Judge for a long moment before asking, "Are you God?"

"Me? I am just your designated Heavenly Judge."

"But you're making the decision."

"No, James . . . you already made the decisions. I judge them because it is my job. And this is my floor. But there are many floors."

"I noticed. That's a pretty long escalator," James says.

"From what I have heard, though, when you are headed on the "down" one . . . Well, let's just say the ride seems very quick."

James considers the implications of that statement.

The Heavenly Judge smiles innocently and prepares the next song. "I would love to hear your third tale, James," he says wearing a smirk that makes James almost suspect he wants a very unfriendly ending for him. But the Judge if for anything is not partial and would be able to assess him perfectly without bias.

"Okay. It was about five years ago. And I was pretty upset that I got passed over for an award nomination. Again. I was busy editing my latest movie in a squat building on a studio backlot."

* * *

Rick is on the couch in front of the TV, sitting with his legs crossed. "Hey! Best Director . . . Get ready. They're about to announce the nominations," he states.

James doesn't look up from his script. He has been disappointed so many times, he almost can't bear to watch again, so he busies himself in his work and tries his level best to avoid it altogether. "At some point, are you going to help me edit this film?"

Rick grabs a big bowl of popcorn and tosses a handful into his mouth. "We got plenty of time for that, Jimbo. Come on, let's watch." Rick is always glued to James; all through the good, bad, and rough times. The two had gone through several risks, all through their film making school to current practice.

"I'm not getting my hopes up again, Rick." James has the mind of a pessimist and most times doesn't expect anything such as a nomination, to avoid disappointment. Rick, on the other hand, has his mind all made up that they will at least make the nominations, and this has kept him going.

"Think positive. It works for me," Rick states.

"Except when whichever skank you're 'dating' this week has to take a pregnancy test."

"Uncool, bro. And Diamond isn't a skank. She's an artiste."

"Pole-dancing isn't an art."

Rick, grinning, says, "My friend, you only say that because you've never seen her dance."

"You're not getting any younger, Ricky. When are you going to stop chasing and settle down?"

"I don't know, bro. I guess when I find the perfect woman for me; I'll be perfect for her too." He looks at the television screen, "Best Director! Here it comes."

James keeps his eyes on the editing, but he simply can't hold in the temptation to cross his fingers in hope and luck. And just as he focuses his mind back on the editing, he has his ears on the sound from the TV. He may not have his eyes there, but his mind is completely on the TV.

He can only imagine the announcer at the podium, getting ready to make the announcement. "Our nominees for best director are . . ."

James pauses his work, head cocked slightly to listen. He closes his eyes and crosses his fingers a little tighter.

"Sorry, bro. That sucks." James hears Rick's voice but doesn't react. It has the same disappointing tone that Rick used when he saw that he and James had to repeat a course in a film class. They both had done poorly, and Rick had checked the results first.

James shrugs and keeps working. He tries to act like it doesn't bother him, but he was surely a better Director than the person announced. The disappointment was etched on his face.

The phone rings but James just continues staring out into nothingness. Rick grabs it, listens a minute, then turns to him.

"Our new producer wants to talk to you." Rick sounds just as disinterested as James when he was making the announcement.

* * *

A secretary opens the door and James enters the office, carrying a script with him. The first thing he sees are sexy high heels attached to a pair of long legs that stretch on for what seems like miles then disappear underneath a short skirt. When he finally looks up and sees the actual face of Studio Vice President, Whitney Kendall, he realizes she is an extremely attractive young woman in her early thirties. Devastatingly beautiful but cold and distant like a star hovering just out of reach. She arches an eyebrow at James.

"Hi there. I'm Jimbo Glass."

"I know. I'm Whitney Kendall. Your new boss."

"What happened to Barry?" he asks.

"He retired." Barry was a good boss. He would review all of James's work and go the extra mile to make the very best selection for the picture. And the way James saw this new boss already, she would not be able to fill Barry's shoes.

"Barry never mentioned that he wanted . . ."

Whitney interrupts him. "I never said he wanted to retire. Barry green-lighted too much crap; out with the old and in with the new."

"But I just gave him a script. I revised the story, and he was considering . . ."

Whitney holds up a script with two fingers, holding it like someone took a crap on it. "You mean this one?"

James nodded, "It's called *Horizontal Rain.*" I want it to be my next picture."

Whitney cradles her head on her hands. "Barry warned me about your little obsession. Nominations must be out. Let me guess. Snubbed again, James?"

"I've made enough crap pictures for this studio."

"Those crap pictures have made us millions." James doesn't know how to hold his anger. He simply tries to bottle his thoughts, maybe later he and Rick could talk about what their next action should be. But for now, he has to try his best to be smart, calm, and exact in his responses.

James starts pacing back-and-forth like a caged tiger. "It'll win every award out there."

"Yeah, it's good, James, but it violates my two cardinal rules: It's depressing as shit, and it's expensive to make. We'll get limited release based on your name recognition. New York, maybe L.A. After that, we'd be lucky to open on five hundred screens. It's going to cost us thirty mil and we'll make seven back if we're lucky."

James protests, "But an award nomination will net..."

"Fine. Another ten million in box office from theatrical re-release plus streaming. Minimal at best from physical copies. Discs are dead, baby. So . . . still not worth it." His new boss sounded all too pessimistic for James's liking and for all he cared, he could easily walk out of here with his picture and get financing for it.

"It is to me. All I'm asking for is a chance. Maybe I can cut some costs by . . ."

Whitney replies with an unfriendly smile, "James, babe. There are two prepositional phrases I know you are unfamiliar with: under budget and on time."

"But I can . . ."

"Were you ever voted homecoming king in school?" She sounds so offensive when she asks the question that he knows she is driving somewhere that he doesn't want her to arrive at. *Why does she want to know about his awards history?* James wonders what she would ask him next.

That comes out of left field and stops him in his tracks. "What? No. Why are you asking me . . ."

"How about college? Join a frat? Run for class president?"

"No, but I don't see . . ."

"The awards you're chasing . . . They're just another popularity contest. And if you think for one second that those little gold statues mean anything more than the paper crown they stick on your head at homecoming, you're deluding yourself." This was it; he didn't like this, and he wasn't trying to get himself into a verbal brawl with her; this was just her first day at work, and it would be a bad idea to piss off this woman on day one.

He quietly replies, "I don't care. I want one. I always have. And this script will get me one."

"The answer's still no, James. And it's not going to change. I've worked too hard to get where I'm at to throw it all away."

"Playing it safe is boring," James tells her.

"You know this business as well as I do. All it takes is one false step to fall of the ledge. And when you're hanging there, the people behind you aren't in line to offer you a helping hand back up."

"I know that, but . . ."

Whitney turns nasty and interrupts him once more, "No buts. They're going to do their best to kick you the hell off. And they'll have your job before you even hit the pavement."

Her face was just a heartbeat away from either a kiss or a punch. But since he entered the office, she had been nothing but offensive and rude. He notices her plump lips and exposed cleavage. James quickly takes his eyes off as he remembers that the woman whose body was trying to seduce him was also trying to stop his picture from being made.

She uncrosses and re-crosses her legs. James can't help but feel drawn to her long legs. Those amazing long legs; he finds himself wanting to slowly run his hands along one of them, up her smooth thigh. He feels hypnotized for a moment before snapping back to reality. James does this a lot; he takes his mind through the motions of acting in a way and then quickly wake himself from it, like shaking off a daydream. If he were lucky enough, the new boss would not notice his eye trailing along her legs; otherwise, he was in . . .

"You can leave now," she says.

Defeated, James heads for the door. He has a feeling he will have a very difficult time working with this new boss. And even if he allowed his mind to run wild, and maybe felt entitled to some sleazy relationship, he knew that he would have to choose between some very difficult options, either to quit his job or stay.

"But you're very talented, James. We're going to have a great future together," the new boss says, but James makes it seem as if he didn't hear her last words. To him, these words did not follow her recent actions. *If she thinks I'm that talented, why not greenlight this picture?* But who was he to call the shots? She may have noticed that she had been too difficult on James, and it was not the best of choices.

He closes his eyes and finds himself back at the disco in the booth.

The Heavenly Judge places the earphones over his ears. "I realized what your stories are missing. A soundtrack!"

"Uh, should I be dancing? Or singing? Or something else?" James asks, confused.

He watches the Judge silently for a moment. Then he gets up and walks around, examining the surroundings while the Judge finishes up his song. James loved doing this whenever he is in a new environment.

"Does everyone wind up here?" James asks.

"What?" The Judge can't seem to hear him through his earphones.

James tries talking a little louder, "I said, does everyone wind up here?" There was no response.

The Judge is suddenly back in his chair. He steeples his hands together, lowering his voice with reverence. "All souls begin here. All souls end up here. To explain how they lived their lives, how they used the time that God gave them. To be judged. Just as you are doing now, James."

"Even if they don't believe?

The Judge appears at his side, joining him for his stroll around the Disco. "Of course. They're just the ones that look the most surprised."

The Judge manipulates the huge screen, which shows an image of the earth again. He then zooms in closer and closer and shows him various images. While looking at the images, James listens to what the Judge is saying. He begins visualizing what he is saying . . .

"God created the Universe, the Heavens, and the Earth, for all his children, all of us. No exception. The only boundaries He set were the oceans...

And yet men drew lines to create divisions and separations and are willing to go to war or use cyberattacks to maintain their supremacy," the Judge says. James could understand why there were walls and fences to demarcate properties and also why many persons would focus on their privacy and how they want to live on themselves. On the screen, James views the entire Earth itself as seen from space, showing continents and water divisions. He gets a view of the German wall, USA borders walls, Gaza fences,

Gets to see hackers sitting in front of multiple laptops conducting cyber-attacks. James realizes they could paralyze electrical grids and planes in the air, move bank balances, access electronic voting machines and anything they wanted to disrupt. They were carrying a war, unnoticed, from anywhere He almost asks the Judge if something can be done to stop the choices of the hackers, but he was paralyzed. with thoughts.

The Judge continues talking in a hypnotic voice, "God created the Earth with an abundance of water, of pure air, and a wonderful variety of climates. And man is destroying the gift of purity and beauty."

Before James on the screen, he can see images of the Grand Canyon, great forests, and a beautiful clear river.

He can also see a river contaminated full of dead fish. He can see a manufacturing plant dumping waste into the oceans, drilling for oil close to the sea, polluting the water with dark ooze.

* * *

"God created man and woman. Men have challenged His magnificent creation and corrupted what God's purpose was. They use and abuse their bodies in so many ways." James wonders how this impacts God's decision in the final judgment. Does He only Judge those who do evil things? Or does He punish all those who damage the earth altogether?

James sees himself teaching piano lessons to Jenna Lynn and Kate painting a picture, together as a family fulfilling God's creation.

He sees an image of drug use and a guy selling drugs to young people on a street corner.

He sees a very young girl, ashamed and forced into prostitution, giving money to her pimp,

He remembers the story Rick told him about a thirteen-year-old girl that was sold for money. He felt terrible. He remembers how Rick mentioned that the girl had no parents, and she was made to stay with her guardian; it was her guardian who sold her off to all these drug dealers for money. The girl had become a sex slave. James remembers how he tried to create a movie that could help enlighten people of the dangers of human trafficking.

James covers his face and eyes with both hands." *I am not letting my mind bring the idea of my Jenna Lynn falling in the hands of a "pervert."*

Drawing him back to the Disco room, the Judge looks him in the eyes.

"God sent his only Son to Earth, to give one message: Love one another as I have loved you. Love ... to oppose the terrible hate on Earth toward others because of their ethnic origin, the color of skin, or how they look or dress.

"The Lord wants everyone to love one another; it's not that they have to make love to each other. How hard is that?"

The Judge's usual mask of indifference slips for a moment, but he quickly regains his composure. He gathers himself and looks at James. "And do you know what pushes people to destroy life, the quality of the Earth we share, create more barriers from the rest, and twist love into a trap? Greed. Greed makes people want more of everything for themselves. Greed makes government extremist and oppressive, employers abusive, and men to sell their soul to the devil.

"Greed is God's enemy. Greed is evil in action."

James suddenly remembers how his aunt had warned him not to be greedy; he remembers a particular instance where she had to make him share his toys so that he could learn that it was best if everyone shared what they had with others because it made them all feel good.

The Judge appears behind him, pacing the floor as he speaks with conviction.

"There is a difference between using your talents for yourself, for your family, for the Glory of God by helping the least of your brothers and using them to cut throats and step on everyone just to get ahead."

The Judge stands in front of James with his phone appearing in his hands, mimicking a child engrossed with the screen. "You see the kids in their little world, obsessively playing those media games that are created to incite their greed at an early age. That's why they spend more time, bet more coins, or seek out more violence. Society trains them to be greedy."

James visualizes a digital slot machine app with the reels spinning numbers and symbols and a shooting game app bloody and violent.

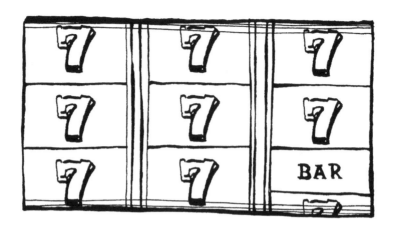

The Judge shakes his head sadly. "Greed pushes kids for more and more. And with that, the future of society will spin out of control like a broken compass unless God and family unity become a priority. It is too late for you, James, but do you understand the message?"

As the Judge continues to talk, James has another vision. He visualizes the Judge's message as if he was about to post it on social media:

"God's presence and family unity beat greed! Share, listen to music, dance, play sports, and pray. Together! And have friends that share your family values, not friends that will cause your demise."

James clicks "Share."

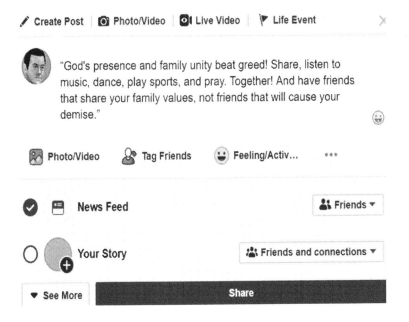

The Judge steeples his fingers under his chin, growing serious. James soon gets up and starts to pace the room. "I understand your message, but why is it too late for me? There are millions of greedy people still alive." James gets angry and yells, "It's not fair."

No one says life was fair. Why would death be any different?" the Judge says, trying to look him in the eyes, but James quickly looks away, unable to meet his gaze. James finds it difficult to understand why the Judge sounds so mean talking about death.

Getting another song ready, the Judge asks, "So, are you ready to continue?" James knows if he continues, it will be a very good experience for him, but he doesn't want to share anything that will negatively impact the decision the Judge will make about him. He feels his heart beat faster when he remembers he has no choice but to be completely honest about all of his experiences.

The music soothes him a bit, and then he agrees to continue, "Sure. It was a couple of years later, I guess. There was a talent show at Jenna's high school. By this time, Kate and I . . . well, our relationship had changed ... a lot."

James recalls the night just like it was yesterday. They were at Jenna Lynn's middle school.

The cafeteria has been converted into the typical recital setup. Tables in the back of the room and all the chairs lined up in rows facing the stage. A piano sit on the stage along with a few sheet music stands. A kid on a flute is wrapping up a rather uneven performance to scattered applause. It is more like a dinner party, and everyone is dressed in an orderly and uniform attire. They have their coats on as they sir arranged in front of the table. The scene reminds James of his high school graduation party.

Kate and James are in the front row, but James seems to be receiving a call. He gets the warning eye from Kate, but he responds with the "just one minute" finger as he walks out of the door. Kate and James usually have heated arguments about calls, and whenever the calls are too long, they end up embarrassing themselves.

Kate is irritated. She looks up and sees Jenna Lynn, now fourteen years old, peeking out from behind the curtain.

Jenna Lynn sees the empty seat next to her mother and holds up her hands, like "Where's Dad?"

Kate mimes talking on a phone with her thumb and forefinger extended by her ear. Disappointed, Jenna Lynn rolls her eyes and disappears back behind the curtain. Kate shakes her head as James returns but doesn't sit down. They have similar arguments at home; every time they discussed attending events that will make Jenna feel special, he comes up with one story or another.

Now, this was going to be a difficult moment for him, as he would have to do a lot to convince Kate of his need to leave the event.

"I got to go, babe. Sorry."

"You never used to miss these shows."

"If I don't go to this meeting and plead my case, they won't greenlight my movie."

Kate looks at her watch, "Kind of late for a meeting, isn't it?" It was nighttime, and even if Kate did not suspect James of having an affair, she had to admit the time was quite late for any meeting of the sort to be held.

"Studio execs are most active at night. Like vampires."

"But this has always been the thing you guys shared. Playing 'Small World' over and over until she got it right. Don't let her down again."

"You know how these things always drag on for hours, and Jenna goes on near the end, right? I'll be back in time." But the look on his face doesn't quite seem to match up with the words coming out of his mouth.

"Do what you have to, James. You always do." She has given up on convincing James to stay. She knows that he never agrees to do something unless he wants to do it. She doesn't want to get in an argument here.

"Sometimes you have to kiss a little ass in this business if you want something done." That was the phrase he usually uses to give himself permission to leave Kate and Jenna.

"Just go then," Kate says.

As the lights start to dim, James begins to kiss Kate, but she angles her head down slightly so he could only kiss her forehead.

"I'll hurry back . . . Maybe I won't miss it."

As he heads out, he sees Kate sitting alone in the darkening room.

"Yes. You will," Kate says sadly.

James knows that leaving her will eventually make her bored of him. She knows that James missing this recital for his meeting will cause another painful wound to their marriage, which is already not in the healthiest of states at the moment.

At the studio, Whitney looks up from the script she's reading at her desk and fixes James with a nasty glare.

"Took you long enough. I should say 'no' and save myself the aggravation."

"What you should be doing is be thanking me for paying your salary. With the box office grosses on my last picture, I deserve this chance." James says.

Whitney throws down James's script *Horizontal Rain* and walks over to him. "You know how much I hate this art-house crap."

"Then don't buy a ticket when the movie comes out," James says the words with anger. He left in the middle of his daughter's event, and the last thing he wants is to come here to deal with this nasty talk from his boss. He feels that he has no other options than to be real to her, at the very least letting her know that he is not out for nonsense.

"James . . ."

"Are you green-lighting it or not?"

Whitney sits on the corner of her desk, crossing her legs and staring hard at James.

"I can think of three other studios that would jump all over the chance to produce the new film by James Glass. Even if it doesn't have seven hundred special effect shots," James continues.

Whitney finally agrees, "Fine. You can start the pre-production next week."

"That's a good decision. One that's going to get us nominated."

"Just wait, James. One day I'll be the head of this studio…"

James cuts her off. "And then you'll steal the ruby slippers, and you and your flying monkeys will rule all of Oz."

James starts walking towards the door. Whitney studies him, arms folded across her chest. "I know what your problem is, James. You're intimidated by strong women.

109

You'd rather be comfortable knowing you have a mousy little wife at home."

"I have no idea what you're talking about." James looks shocked at her comment about his wife. Her words cross his heart in a way he never expected, *why was she referring to his wife?*

"What happened to the man who stood in my office a year ago and told me that playing it safe was boring?"

Still standing at the door, James notices Whitney still studying him, almost as if he is prey, her arms folded tightly across her chest.

"You think I'm a bitch . . ." she says slyly.

James already has a hand on the doorknob, but he hasn't started turning it. "I know you are."

Whitney states, "And it turns you on, doesn't it?"

James stares hard at the door, fighting the urge. "I should go."

"You probably should. But you won't."

James slowly turns his head back toward Whitney, getting another eyeful of leg . . .

* * *

Jenna Lynn steps out on stage and sits at the piano. She is suddenly bathed in the spotlight. She starts to play and sing in a beautiful lilting voice. It's obvious that she has talent, even at a young age. Even as she performs, however, you can see her eyes narrowing in the glare of the stage lights as she scans the crowd.

It's not stage fright, though, she is already much too confident to doubt herself much. She finds Kate in the crowd. Kate gives her a little wave and an encouraging smile. Jenna

Lynn's eyes fall on the empty seat beside Kate. Her voice cracks, and she suddenly stops singing. With a strangled cry, she jumps off the piano bench and runs offstage.

It is a painful experience for her; she has practiced and planned in the hope that James would be present, only for her to check while on stage and realize her father was nowhere to be found. She ran out in pain, trying so hard to decide what to do next. Her bright red gown flowing behind her like a dangling rose to fall from a tall branch. She almost misses her step as she runs off the stage. But nothing bothers her more than the fact that James's presence is absence from her event.

* * *

James remains at Whitney's office door . . . is still at the door. He visualizes himself running toward Whitney, grabbing her face in his hands and starting to kiss her passionately; he plays through his mind how he would try to later convince Kate why he stayed out so late in the office . . .

Instead, James watches Whitney saunter over to him. She pushes him back against the door, shutting it. Her body presses against his. The struggle must be clear on his face; with his eyes rolling around trying to catch his breath, he was never prepared for something like this.

"We could do great things if we work together, James. Think about it. We'll run this town. Make millions. Win awards. Let's make our new partnership official."

Whitney kisses him forcefully. He resists at first then starts kissing her back urgently. She starts to wrap her legs around him, and then they stumble into her desk. Whitney nibbles on his ear. They both are entangled, body-to-body like one creature with one purpose: pleasure.-

"When I first came to Hollywood, I was eighteen and an intern at a studio. The VP I was working for back then made it clear that he was going to help my career if I slept with him, so I did."

A moment of pain flashes in her eyes and on her face, so fast it'd be easy to miss. Then the mask quickly returns. She was a victim of circumstance and of a bad boss. Maybe she would have been able to still achieved her goal while resisting the offer from her VP, but how could she when he held all the power and control? "I found out I had what it took to make it."

James already had all he could take up to that point. He eagerly pushes her back against the desk.

Turned on now, Whitney lets out a little moan and tugs violently at his belt. Everything is set for a quick moment of pleasure; something that he knows will cost him a lot if Kate finds out. His heart races hard against his chest as he takes his mind through the act of doing this act.

"And I thought you hated me . . ." James manages to mutter, yet he knows that she was planning this. Maybe she had been focused on this since she set her eyes on him.

As James's pants hit the ground, along with his keys and his cell phone, he pushes Whitney against the desk. He hears her moan.

Suddenly, his cell phone vibrates on the floor as he receives an incoming call. The caller ID reads KATE . . .

* * *

A little while later, James hurries back to the school cafeteria, but the recital is over. The place is empty except for some workers in the back, collecting chairs. He knows that neither Jenna Lynn nor Kate will take it lightly with him. He has a lot to explain to them. He sits beside the hall, on the pavement and thinks of how he had betrayed the trust of his little girl.

"Damn," he says. "Why did I do this?"

He decides to head home. As he walks into the kitchen, he finds Kate sitting at the table. There's half a bottle of red wine in front of her. She doesn't even look up at him. She usually will drink to burn off the anger whenever she quarrels with James. But today, there was no quarrel, what had happened was worse.

"I guess you got stuck in something at the office, huh?" Kate slurs her words a bit.

"I'm sorry." James pulls up a chair and turns it around to sit backward on it. He shifts his eyes to the bottle of wine.

"I thought you were going to cut down on that," James mentions as if he has no idea why Kate is drinking so much alcohol of late.

Kate still refuses to make eye contact. "That's funny. I was about to ask you the same thing. You smell like perfume."

"It's probably yours."

Kate repeats the word, tasting it on her lips as if it is a fine wine, "Probably."

"I mean it must be yours. I'm just tired."

"Yeah. Me too," Kate says.

James looks around, "Is she in her room?" he says, asking about Jenna.

"That's where she usually goes to cry when you let her down."

And because James gives no response, Kate speaks up again, "She didn't perform. She came out and started singing, but when she saw you weren't there, she just ran off stage." Kate watches as James face changes. His eyes widen; he never imagined that his absence would lead to something like that.

Kate refills her glass, emptying the bottle. She takes her glass and stands up, walking with an unsteady gait. "It's a shame . . . I think she sings even better than she plays piano now. She's got a beautiful voice. Maybe one day you'll take the time to listen to it again."

Kate pauses next to James, leans down close by his ears and says quietly, "And I didn't wear any perfume tonight."

James manages to keep an impassive pose as he hears the door slam as Kate walks out. He shuts his eyes. He feels the pain of Kate and Jenna Lynn. He can only imagine the humiliation Jenna Lynn had gone through.

Later that night, James softly knocks on the bedroom door. "Jenna? Jenna Lynn? Honey, open the door, please."

No answer. He rests a hand on the handle as he knocks again and to his surprise, the door opens. He peeks inside. He never felt Jenna would open the door. A few nights ago, when he knocked after forgetting her rehearsals, she didn't open the door. He thought today would be the same, but . . .

Even from the doorframe, he can see the room looks ransacked. Drawers are open or pulled out entirely from the dresser. The closet is also a mess. Discarded clothes everywhere, many more taken. A sock here and there ... and the bedroom window is open just enough for someone small to crawl through. She's gone. His eyes open wide.

"Kate!" James stands in the doorway, feeling too terrified to enter Jenna Lynn's bedroom. But where had she gone?

He hears Kate's footsteps behind him and hears her gasp; the wine glass in her hand slips from her grip and hits the ground in shatters, spraying red wine across the tile floor like a bloodstain . . .

* * *

Back in the Disco room, James opens his eyes, shocked to see a woman in a gown in her forties, standing out on the dance floor alone. He quickly does a double-take on what he was seeing. She looks very confused.

"Where am I?" she says as she looks around. "This is so beautiful."

James keeps staring at the woman. The Judge does not look the slightest bit concerned. As if this sort of thing happens all the time . . . The lights in the room flare up brightly; a rainbow of colors. The music becomes quite loud, and suddenly, the woman is gone. The lights return to normal, and the music dims.

James scans the room, but there's no trace that the woman was ever there. The Judge stands alone on the dance floor.

"They always remember my lights."

"I guess it wasn't her time?" James asked.

The Judge takes his seat again. "The hands of the clock do not move here, James. Eternity is free of such constraints. Heaven is always now, the true day by day, living fully." Life is constantly and always the right time.

"So, was that woman we saw dead? Or not?" James tries to confirm what he thought had happened to the woman. He looks to the Judge for a response.

"Yes. And yes." The Judge clicks off the remote.

Feeling a little envious, he says, "She's lucky . . . to get a second chance, I mean." James thinks maybe he should have been given a second chance too and not just brought in here without the opportunity of going back.

There is a moment of silence, and then the Judge reappears in his seat and asks:

"What happened with Kate?"

James's expression changes when he is asked the question. He doesn't like the fact that he has to relive all the terrible times he had spent with Kate here again. He looks down as he replies to the Judge.

"We had already stopped trying to save our marriage. And Whitney was so exciting, we . . ."

"Wait, I need a great song for this," the Judge says while searching for a tune. "So many to choose from . . . Aha!" He plays a calm song, and although James had heard the song before, he can't recall the title of the song and the person who had sung it.

"We had fun together . . . we went out to dinners. We shared a passion for making movies and for making love all night. Everything was going so well. Until one day ..."

James finally began to keep late nights; each time he came home, he would meet Kate seated, drunk in the dining room. Sometimes, he just walked past her, some other times, he moved over to where she was seated and took her into her room. James was between two fixes, he did what he did, but his heart was bearing down heavily on him.

James remembers a few fleeting moments of the first days Whitney and him were together. They sat at an expensive restaurant, toasting, laughing, and kissing. He and Whitney in the editing room, making out on the couch as one of James's movies plays in the background; he and Whitney making love in her bedroom—with Whitney on top of course.

As they finish, Whitney lays back in the bed. She glances at James, looking at him in a way that tells him she must have had something ominous planned. Whitney has not been a very sincere person, and James knows it.

"I have a story to tell you," Whitney says.

James sits up looking straight at her; he wants to be sure that he gets the full story she is about to share to him.

"Ever since I was born, I have had a tense look. And right from age four, I could look into the eye of an adult and cause that electric bolt to make him shake for fear. Even if I didn't do it on purpose, I had this bold look in my eyes. However, it wasn't until I was twelve that I learned about my facial uniqueness; it was only then that I used it for my benefit to get people to submit to my will."

James listened as he tried to understand what she meant.

"But don't be scared, James, I am not doing that to you. James, you are the one true person I have ever loved. It would make me so happy if you got a divorce so we could get married."

James gets up and sits in the "foot of the bed", knowing that's never going to happen.

"I want you to get a divorce," she says again after another long pause of silence from James.

"I can't do that, Whit. I'm sorry. Come on, we both knew that . . ."

Whitney abruptly sits up in bed, pulling on a nightshirt to cover herself. "Get out."

James sits up on one elbow, confused. "What?"

Whitney walks to the bathroom. "We're done." The door slams behind her. It was all Whitney had wanted; she wanted to get James to the place where he would not be able to reject her proposal to ask for a divorce.

The Heavenly Judge raises his eyebrows at that particular section of the story. James just ends it and watches him for a moment without saying a word.

"We had such a good time together. I thought she was just looking for fun, but she wanted more." James sighs. "So much more than I was willing . . . or able . . . to give her."

James pauses for a moment before continuing, "You know, it's funny. At the time, I only thought about how nasty she was to everyone. I guess I didn't realize it was even possible to hurt her."

James cradles his head in his hands. "God, I've done so much in my life that I never apologized for."

Filled with guilt, James locks eyes with the Heavenly Judge, who says slowly, "Are you ready?"

James is surprised by the way the Judge never offers any comments on the stories he's been telling so far, even if he has done terrible things in them. He hopes that these stories do not end up leaving him with the worst possible ending for his time here. "Do you have a song?"

The Heavenly Judge is suddenly standing. He waves a hand like a conductor, calling for the orchestra's attention. "I have many songs. Regretfully, I cannot write on my own."

James nods in understanding and closes his eyes. "I'll tell you about the day I finally got nominated for an award, for my film *Horizontal Rain*. It was supposed to have been the best day of my life." He laughed. "Then I got a call from Kate asking me to meet her for breakfast. I thought she wanted to congratulate me . . ."

* * *

They meet in a hip cafe in LA with a lot of Hollywood talent around. James sits at a table alone across from Kate, on her cell phone. Neither of them is happy. Kate has this sad, soulful look that comes from the pain she has suffered in his absence. She loved James with all her heart only to be left for a woman who he was never going to be serious with, but just wanted to advance his career.

"How's Jenna doing?" James tries to make conversation.

Kate ignores him as she finishes up her conversation on the phone. She puts her phone down but still does not answer him.

"Did you hear me?"

"She's getting by; she's in high school now. Everything in her life is changing. Why don't you call yourself some time and ask her?"

"Yeah. I know. I've just been so busy with work . . ." It is harsh how James sounds.

Why are you too busy for your daughter? Kate wonders, looking surprised by his comments. She reflects on the man she first fell in love with, the man who delivered Jenna into this world. He wouldn't have disregarded their daughter—or so she thought.

"Of course, you are. When you walk down that red carpet with your girlfriend Whitney, I hope you still think it was all worth it."

"What are you talking about . . ."

"You know, if you had gotten drunk and had sex with her one time, I probably could have forgiven it." Kate looks straight in his eyes as she makes these accusations. It was high time they talked about this, and even if James seemed busy, she was ready to make him come to his senses.

"I . . ." Before he can continue talking, Kate cuts him off.

"But to carry on a whole affair with that whore. I can't . . ."

"Whitney and I broke up. She wanted me to get a divorce."

Kate gives a bitter laugh. "Wow. Whitney and I finally agree on something."

Kate pulls some paperwork out of her purse and pushes it toward James. James looks down at them . . . divorce papers. His eyes pop out like some cartoon toad; he looks miserable, he never wanted that, but it seems he took too long to realize his mistake.

James looks back up at Kate, completely shell-shocked. "But . . . I thought. I mean, I was hoping we could get back together now."

"Oh, now. Now. Now that we've been separated for almost a year. Now that you're done sticking your dick into someone else. Now that she's done with you. I should take you back?"

Kate stands up. "Did you love her?"

James doesn't answer her for a moment. "No, but I thought I did."

Kate nods silently. "Here's your new 'now,' James. Now you need to sign these."

Kate storms out of the café. That leaves a clear space for James to see right to the next table, where a stunningly beautiful young woman is seated alone. She is sipping coffee and pursuing a Hollywood Trade Paper. She raises an eyebrow as she notices him staring and flashes a quick smile with pursed lips.

James visualizes the woman on a movie set. He is filming a scene with her as the lead actress. And then giving direction to her on the scene . . .

The woman must have sensed him still gazing to her as she glances back up. The waitress delivers two orders of pancakes, putting one down in front of him and one at the now vacant seat across for Kate. James stares at the food cooling on the table.

James pulls out his cell phone and scrolls down to Whitney. He dials her number. The phone rings and rings; then voicemail. He hangs up without leaving a message. When he looks back up, the intriguing woman is now staring hard at him.

"Sorry to keep staring, but aren't you Jimbo Glass?" she asks. James looks on as she talks. He is rather surprised that she identified him. Maybe he really has become popular over the years!

He can't help but smile at the recognition and nod. He runs his finger through his hair, trying to be presentable. "No problem. Happens all the time . . ."

"Oh my God, I'm sure you get tired of hearing this, but I love your movies."

James knows that if he doesn't control this discussion, it might lead him to another situation that he may not like. James smiles as he watches her, practically beaming at the compliments. "Thank you, uh . . ."

The woman gets up and walks over with her coffee, leaning against the table to present the best view of her ample cleavage. "Sage Skye."

"Sage. That's a great name. Fits you. And no, I never get tired of hearing that. Would you care to join me? Lotta pancakes to eat by myself."

"I would, sugar. I just love pancakes."

Sage sits down across from him, smiling. He remembers the divorce papers in front of him, and he puts his breakfast plate right on top to conceal them. James recollects how he hid his face in the library just so he could escape the security man chasing him, that was the first day he met Kate.

"So, what do you do?" James asks her.

Sage laughs, "Struggling actress. One day though, I'd like to just be an actress. You know, without the struggling part."

"Have you been in anything I might have seen?"

"Well, my last film was an independent, so probably not . . ."

James laughs, enjoying having a conversation instead of an argument.

"But now I'm ready to move on to bigger and better . . . awards and fame and some paparazzi hiding out in my landscaping. Maybe a reality show." With a little laugh, she adds, "Can you understand that, Mr. Glass?"

"I sure can, Sage. And please, call me Jimbo."

"Well, congratulations on your nomination . . . Jimbo. I can imagine this is a very happy day for you."

James glances down at the corner of the divorce papers sticking out from under his dish. "You know, it should be, right? Anyway, I'm enjoying the company."

Sage smiles, warmly.

"Hey, I'd like to celebrate my nomination, it took long enough to get one finally. Would you care to join me? I mean, if you don't have plans, tonight."

Sage smiles from ear to ear. "I've got an audition this afternoon, but after that . . . Nope, no plans at all."

Sage pulls out a pen and goes to grab the edge of the paperwork that he was hiding under his plate. She realizes that they are divorce papers. She pauses a moment . . . Then casually rips off the corner of the divorce paper and scribbles her number on it. Sage slides it over with one manicured finger and an incredible smile. Flirty, sexy, and confident. Thinking: *This is all mine.* "Call me." She leaves the table and heads for the door.

He seizes the opportunity to check out her statuesque figure and . . .

He imagines what it would be like back at Sage's apartment. He is behind Sage, pulling her back into him; he slides his hand from her neck to her shoulders and then her back, where he hurriedly begins unzipping her dress. Sage moans and lets the dress fall away, reaching for him . . .

James has a mind that is always connecting dots both between others and moments in time.

He stares at her number a moment; then he pulls out his cell phone to enter it into his contacts. As he does so, he receives a call. The caller ID reads KATE. His finger pauses over the answer key as he decides whether to take the call or not.

He raises his head and sees Sage. She gives him a wink and a little wave as she exits the cafe. James has always seemed to find himself between ladies, and this has been a problem for him. If he were ever going to remain faithful, then he should probably just ensure he reduces his exposure to other ladies who end up taking his attention from Kate.

That's what I should probably do, James thinks. James feels a slow smile build on his face. James simply declines Kate's call and allows it to go to voicemail.

Later that afternoon, he finds himself seated on one of Sage's couches in her home. Both of them have a script in hand. There is a bottle of wine and two glasses on the table.

"That's a great scene," Sage comments.

"It's in my new film. I start shooting at the end of the year. You really should audition," James encourages her.

"I've been getting acting lessons here and there when money allows."

"Listen, I know a great guy. Old school character actor. He owes me a few favors. I could call one in for you, let him teach you some really good stuff."

Sage runs a hand across his legs. "You are so sweet. It must have been fate I ran into you. 'Cause I've known you all of a couple of hours and you're already changing my little life for the better."

James takes a drink of wine and grin. "I'll set it up. No worries. You know, in my experience the thing you got to nail as an actress is being able to respond truthfully to a given moment." James thinks he sounds so wise as he says that, locking eyes with the song starlet, trying to make a connection through their eyes, the windows to the soul.

Sage picks up her glass, running a well-manicured finger over the rim playfully. "How so?"

"Your attention should always remain on your co-actor and what he or she is preparing to say or do."

Sage seems to already have that down as she gazes longingly at James. She puts her glass back down on the table. They both know they are at the edge of becoming very intimate, it is a gradual process, and for once he thinks that he will not be able to go back to Kate even if she accepts him.

"You get a far less self-conscious performance and come across much more authentic."

"I've never been the self-conscious type," she says.

Sage climbs on top of him, passionately kisses his neck. They are all over each other. James momentarily breaks the embrace. He grasps her shoulders to turn her around, and then anxiously begins unzipping her dress. Sage lets out a moan as the dress fall from her shoulders.

As James opens his eyes again, he is back in the Disco room with the Judge standing behind him.

"It appears that you have three very interesting candidates, James. Picking one with whom to spend eternity will be no simple task." James looks at himself and thinks his brain will never understand who to pick when it comes down to any of the three ladies in his life. But he surely knows where his heart lies.

James shakes his head, feeling very despondent. "But I wonder if I'll even get the chance to choose . . ."

The Judge is at the multimedia screen, sliding a hand across the screen. He zooms in and out while checking on various people still on Earth. James has no idea of the location he is checking.

"I think that a good arbitrator never passes judgment until all the facts have been presented."

James walks over to the Judge; he doesn't look at the screen, but rather the Judge's reaction to what he's seeing.

"Why do you enjoy this so much?"

Without taking his eyes off the screen to look at James, the Judge replies, "I love to hear good stories as much as I love to listen to good music. It is the drama, I suppose, of what people do and why they do it. It fascinates me so. The same reasons that have motivated a crowd to silence their own stories for a time and just . . . listen."

It finally dawns on me, "You were never alive, were you?"

The Heavenly Judge doesn't answer at first, he merely continues to study the large screen. "Not in the way you experience it, no."

"That seems pretty unfair . . . I mean, walk in the shoes of the people you judge for a day. See if you always make the right decision."

The Judge finally turns to face James. "If you know what the right decision is, then surely you must know when you choose to make the wrong one?"

James looks down. "It's not always clear at the time."

The Judge is back at his soundboard, searching through his musical choices. "Tell me about it."

James nods while walking back over to get comfortable. He leans back toward the microphone. "About a year ago, Sage became my live-in girlfriend. She was visiting the set of my new movie . . ."

Sage and James walk hand-in-hand through the set. They stop at his Director's Chair, which reads JAMES GLASS across the back.

"Pretty cool, huh?"

"Wow, Jimbo. I've never been to a big-budget movie set before. Thank you so much." James always hears that from those who visit him, yet it never fails to inflate his ego.

"Here, why don't you take her for a spin?" he offers in gentlemanly fashion.

"Really? Is it okay?"

"Of course, I'm the director!"

Sage wriggles into the seat and puts her arms on the armrests. "This is so incredible," she says as she looks around. "But where is everybody?"

"Finishing up pre-production. We don't start principal photography until tomorrow. A few of the principals are already on set."

James hands her a script.

"What's this?" she asks.

"A little surprise. Your lines are highlighted."

Sage lights up like a Christmas tree. "Are you serious?"

"Congratulations on your first major movie role, Miss Skye."

Sage squeals in delight. She wraps her arms around James and pulls him close. He feels her press hard against his body. James doesn't want her to back out too fast and keeps her held tightly for a long moment, drinking in her perfume and the floral smell of her hair.

"Do you think I'm ready?" Sage asks.

"I know you are. Baby, you're going to be a star."

He holds up a pair of keys. Sage looks at him questioningly. "Every star needs her trailer, of course," he says.

Sage snatches the keys and squeals in delight. As they kiss, he hears a new voice joining the conversation. James wasn't expecting anybody; he knew that his workers would not be done with pre-production already. As such, the voice in the background was more than a little of a surprise to him.

"I didn't realize your new film was a porno." James's eyes pop out as he sees his daughter walking towards them.

Seventeen-year-old pop star Jenna Lynn Glass sneers her hello to Sage and turns to face James.

"Jenna! What are you doing here?"

"Took the words right out of my mouth."

"Hey, James," Jenna says and looks over to direct some venom at Sage. "Congrats on sleeping your way into show business."

Sage stands there looking confused. Since James didn't discuss his daughter often, Sage practically did not know who she was. "You don't know the first thing about me."

"Don't care."

With a warning in his tone of voice, James says, "Jenna, I know you're not happy that Sage is my girlfriend. But whether you like it or not . . ."

"I'll go with 'not.'"

"You will treat her with respect." James finishes his sentence. But it doesn't have any impact. There is nothing he can say to Jenna that will convince her to treat Sage with respect. She never liked the fact that James had left Kate.

"Don't start trying to talk to me like a father, James. You're about four years too late for that."

"That's not fair," Sage interjects.

James quickly steps in trying to defuse this situation before it gets any worse. "I'm really glad to see you, baby. But what do you want?" he says that trying to win over Jenna, but he barely knows his own daughter anymore.

Jenna Lynn gives him a hurt look. She has experienced so much pain as a result of his actions. And so far, she has made up her mind to hold him accountable for all that he did to her. All the disappointment she has felt toward James has piled up over the years, and she seems unwilling to accept any kind of relationship from him that doesn't involve money.

"Jenna, the only time you call or come by is when you need something," James says, quite correctly.

"Fine. I'll get to the point then. A lot of doors have opened since I almost won Pop Star . . ."

"Didn't you come in, like, ninth?" Sage says with spite.

Jenna looks at Sage, "Nine! Wow, I had no idea you could count that high. And I came in seventh so suck a toe."

"Jenna!" James warns her.

"I'm supposed to fly out to New York this Saturday. I have an audition for some big-time record producers and . . ."

"And?"

"And they sent me tickets in coach! Coach, James! Coach!"

James pinches the bridge of his nose and sighs. "So, what exactly do you need from me?" James asks with a slightly raised tone, his eyebrow already raised, his impatience already hitting the roof.

"Are you serious? I can't travel with the general public. Do you know how many people will be trying to get an autograph?"

"Why? Are you flying with somebody famous?" Sage chimes in. Sage was just supposed to shut up; Jenna would not take any comments from her lightly—except that Sage was up for a war of words, ready to join the type of verbal battle for which Jenna was ready.

Jenna looks Sage up and down. "Listen up, Barbie . . . You really should sue your plastic surgeon for crimes against my eyeballs."

"Sugar, I understand you resent me for being with your father, and I'm trying to be nice here, but you aren't making it easy."

Jenna did not want anything from her because she felt Sage was yet another obstacle to her parents being together again.

"I guess I like making things difficult," Jenna confirms. "I must get that from James."

Sage squeezes James's arm. "You know what? I think I'm going to take a walk around this incredible set." Sage shakes her keys happily. "And go check out my new trailer." It was too early to let out the fact that James just got her a new home away from home.

"Something wrong with the one you live in now?" Jenna chuckles.

"Sold it. I just moved in with Jimbo. I'll leave you two alone."

"Wish it was permanently," Jenna leaves Sage with one last snide comment.

"Thanks, Sage," James says, relieved. He already knew that he would not be able to contain the two of them in the same room. Sage's decision to leave was great news for him.

As they walk toward James's office to continue their conversation, Jenna Lynn watches Sage leave and then turns back to James. "Shouldn't you be abandoning me to chase after her? That's what you normally do. Oh, wait, Mom's not here, so I guess it just wouldn't be the same."

James starts to snap off a response, but that one hits the bullseye. And hurts. He takes a deep breath to try and calm down, then he says softly, "How's she doing?"

"Out living her life. Are you going to upgrade my ticket to first class or not?"

"I just want to know."

"I just want an answer."

"How much?"

"Nine hundred," she says, while extends her hand to get the money coming from James wallet. She knows he cannot resist her smile.

"Fine. Here is what you need. Look, it's been way too long. Why don't you have dinner with me before you go?"

"Sorry, James. I'm really busy right now. Maybe next time." Jenna Lynn said while placing money in her purse.

She gives James a quick peck on the cheek and starts walking away. He stares after her, struck with a sudden bout of deep regret.

Upset, James asks, "Can you at least ask her to call me? Or stop by? I don't even know where she's working." James mentions this as if he wouldn't be able to find out if he wants to.

Jenna Lynn pretends she doesn't hear James. And then she's gone . . .

* * *

"I just don't understand why."

"I told you, baby. Sometimes instead of why, you got to ask why not."

"I am loving the notion of my script coming alive," James comments. "Good. Sage, just a touch more emotion. A little more pain in your voice."

Sage nods and tries again. "I . . . I don't understand. Why?"

"Nice," James approves.

"You want us to do the kiss, James?"

James winks at Sage, "Yeah, let's see if you guys have any chemistry. Take it from your line, Ken." James knows that it will be difficult for Sage to give her best try on this action. But he still tries to convince them to do just exactly what he wants them to do.

"Sometimes instead of why, you got to just ask why not." Ken Darvin leans in and pulls Sage into a kiss. But Sage is uncomfortable with James watching. It goes on for a moment, and then James makes the call, "Cut!"

Thinking for a moment, James says, "Not terrible, but . . . Sage, I don't think there was enough passion in that one."

James could see Ken looking eager to try again. "Again?"

He gives Sage some more direction. "Okay, Sage. Find the truth at the moment. Kiss him as if you were kissing me."

Sage nods, a bit shyly and then looks over at Ken Darvin with a grin.

"Ken . . . line."

"Sometimes instead of why, you got to just ask why not."

Ken Darvin pulls Sage into a kiss that is much hotter and more passionate than the last one. This is clearly how Sage wanted to kiss him all along but was holding back.

"Cut. Much better. Nice job, Sage. I knew a great actress was hiding in there."

Sage replies but glances at Ken Darvin as she answers, "You just bring it out in me, I guess."

James phone rings. "Hello?"

He hears his daughter's voice on the other end. "Mom got a spot at that art studio over on Polk and Tyler. Her painting took first place. Don't forget to congratulate her."

Without waiting for a response, he hears Jenna put the phone down.

"Who was that?" Sage asks.

He shrugs. "The wrong number, I guess," James lies. He doesn't want Sage to feel threatened. But was this the best move to make in a time when he needed to tell the truth?

He checks his watch. "I've got an appointment at the studio. Why don't you guys run some more lines?"

"Sounds good, Jimbo," Ken confirms.

James gives Sage a quick peck. "I'll be back in a bit. Call me if you need anything."

Sage grins, "Don't you worry about me, sugar. I'll be fine."

As he leaves the trailer, he thinks he catches Sage eyeing Ken . . . but since he doesn't have anything much to fight for, he just continues to go where he is supposed to be.

In her studio space, Kate is seated at an easel, putting some finishing touches on a lovely painting of a stormy horizon.

A museum curator in his late thirties stands behind her, arms folded, watching her work. He leans close to her . . . his breath is tickling her neck.

"Amazing, Katie," he says.

"Thank you, Arthur," she says. Kate told herself she had the right to allow someone to get close to her, and she knew Arthur had a crush on her for some time. Anyway, she would not even care if James was here watching him get so close to her. For all she cared, James never existed; she had left all the pain he had caused her behind and was moving forward with her life.

"Amazing! You're making my decision to let you debut your work at my new exhibit make me seem like a genius."

She blows at a long strand of hair that has fallen in her eyes. Her face is beaming with pride. "I can't even believe the premiere is this weekend. I'm hurrying to get this piece done." Kate feels so comfortable around him. She loves the way he was calm, nice, and easy. He only wants her to paint things that she is interested in . . .

"I have faith in you. I'm not sure which is more beautiful, the art or the artist."

Kate giggles at that. Her cheeks lighten up as she continues to place her focus on the art that lies in front of her. She has learned over time to give more attention to her art and a little less to men.

"You know, the museum is throwing a little soiree tomorrow night to celebrate our new China exhibit. Drinks and finger foods. Why don't you join me?"

Kate considers this. "Maybe I will." She has this touch that makes her seem in control whenever she talks up an idea to anyone. She may have agreed to go to the event, yet she would not be held responsible if she did not show up.

The strand of hair falls again. Kate starts to reach for it but now has paint on her hands. She glances at the curator flirtatiously. "Arthur, can you give me a hand?" He loves Kate, so he would absolutely make the effort to help her. He had made some slight advances toward her several times, and it helped her self-confidence in the periods when she was feeling lonely.

James watches from the entrance as Kate asks Arthur to help her with a strand of hair. Kate turns to face the curator. They are very close. He brushes a loose strand of hair from her face. This is something that James should be doing, but here is someone else taking his place, and it hurts him so bad.

James can visualize the way she looks up at Arthur and slowly wraps her arms around him. Their faces move closer, lips almost brushing. Without hesitating, James comes running over, face twisted in a fury. He punches the curator in the face; over and over again. He is pummeling the man like a punching bag until his face is swollen and cut and bleeding.

James snaps back to the moment and wonders absently if he has made Kate feel less valued during their marriage. But he can't do that right now. He has let Kate down for so long that it would not be right to fight for her. *Would it?* James wonders. She doesn't need him anymore, not for anything, she has served him divorce papers . . .

Regaining control over his thoughts, he looks at the scene before him. The curator grins and reaches out to gently tuck Kate's errant lock of hair back behind her ear.

"Thanks."

As if feeling someone staring her, Kate looks up and notices James. Even from over there, she can see the jealousy flare up in his eyes. She doesn't mind at first, but later it will get to her, she really loved James, but in the end, he had disappointed her over and over again.

"James!" she says, "What are you doing here?"

Arthur quickly straightens up. He knows from the look of things that he is not welcome. He debates whether to wait and listen to their conversation or simply leave. Staying might not be okay, though, so he awaits confirmation.

Kate looks at the curator. "Thanks again. I'll see you tomorrow night."

Arthur sighs, grateful but slightly disappointed. That was an easy way out for him. As Kate dismisses him, which he was happy she did, he plans on asking her about James when he meets her tomorrow.

The curator nods and quickly exits the studio, flashing a quick "hello" smile at James. James tries to make the man feel uncomfortable, looking at him in an unwelcoming manner. James makes sure to return the "hello" with obvious insincerity.

"Who was that guy?" James asks Kate as the curator leaves. Kate looks up, trying to understand why James would even bother to show concern. As far as Kate knew, he was never interested in her after he met Whitney. *So why now?* she thought.

"Arthur is the curator of the Bella Art Museum. Not that it's any of your business."

"Yeah, he seems friendly."

"Oh, it's okay that you've moved on to some parasite wannabe actress girlfriend, but I should stay in mourning the rest of my life. Maybe enter the convent?"

"I didn't come here to argue," James mentions, trying very hard to be formal.

"Why did you come here? Finally bringing me our divorce papers?"

"My lawyer's still looking them over." James is certain the files are somewhere in his office and not with any lawyer. He simply wants Kate to finally listen to him.

"Uh-huh. Sure. It's only been a few years since we separated. He must be very thorough."

"He better be for the money I'm paying him."

Kate asks him again, "Then why are you here?" She was not giving him any chances; she suddenly felt the old fire rising and wanted to do away with him as quickly as possible.

"I just wanted to congratulate you. And you haven't been returning my phone calls." James had tried several times to reach out to her, but she wouldn't take the calls. They both had enough time to do whatever they pleased, ignoring the feelings of the other person.

"Is there anything else you wanted? I'm kind of busy." Kate's word conveys her annoyance, but James ignores that. He focuses on being nice without letting any of her words get to him.

"Jenna stopped by the set today. Of course, that was because she needed money to fly to New York. I don't understand why she only . . ."

"Yes, you do."

There's a long, awkward moment as neither James nor Kate knows what to say. Kate turns back to her artwork.

James turns to leave but stops. "You've always been a wonderful artist. It's good to see you get recognized for it finally."

Kate stares at James for a moment, surprised. "Thanks. It was good to see you."

Kate adds a brushstroke, then turns and says, "James, I . . ."

But James pretends not to hear her as he walks out. Maybe he felt it was his time to ignore her, but deep down, he really wanted to know what Kate was about to tell him.

* * *

Suddenly, he is back at the Disco with the Judge, pacing the floor.

"Why does everything seem so much clearer when you're looking back at it instead of living it?" James asks.

The Heavenly Judge studies him, approving of his new attitude. It is good that James is realizing what he has been doing wrong and how he has to learn from the past. In the Judge's experience, that is the most difficult lesson for human beings to learn and even harder to fully understand. Turning the mirror of self-evaluation on yourself is a challenge few are willing to undertake, and even fewer can meet with success.

"It would appear that we have come full circle, James."

"You were right. Telling these stories has helped me. A lot. It's helped me decide who I want to be with . . . in Heaven. Hopefully."

"Well said. I can see why you are such a renowned storyteller, James," says the Judge. "Now then . . . you have spun so many tales for me thus far: some sounded fairly good, and some did not seem to go in your favor."

James nods and eagerly takes his seat. He leans forward now, much more excited to continue.

"So, we're all tied up."

"That leaves one story left to tell. And it has now become the most important of all. For it will now determine your fate."

"Lucky Number Seven . . ."

"I have the perfect song." The Judge smiles, leans his head back, and closes his eyes. His foot taps along. The Judge seems disinterested in how exactly James spends his eternity; it seems the Judge is more concerned with how he can reach a decision from all of James's experiences.

* * *

James moves closer to the microphone while licking his lips.

He is sitting in his car, looking at the guard gate into his old residential community. The engine is off. So is the radio. Alone with his thoughts, he takes a deep breath and opens the car door. James's cell phone buzzes. He looks down, and the caller ID shows him that it's Sage calling. He doesn't answer. He sends the call to voicemail instead.

The moment of truth . . .

He looks at the divorce papers in his hands, pauses, and places them into a manila folder. He turns the car back on and drives toward the guard gate—the guard glances into the car and smiles.

"Hey there, Mr. Glass. Haven't seen you around here in a while."

"Could you do me a favor?"

"Sure, Mr. Glass. What do you need?"

He hands the guard the manila folder. "Can you throw these out for me?" James believes he will not need the papers anymore since he has decided to plead with Kate to accept him back, which would be a difficult decision for Kate knowing exactly how much pain he has put her through.

A few minutes later, Kate opens the front door and sees James standing there. Jenna Lynn crosses her arms, guarded.

He pulls a bouquet of sunflowers from behind his back and presents them to Kate.

"My favorite; you still remember?"

"Of course, . . . I guess I just forgot how much I enjoyed giving them to you."

James glances over, "Hey, Jenna."

Jenna looks over at Kate, eyebrows raised. "Wow, I guess I lost that bet, Mom."

She looks at him, "I never thought you'd show up here." She had expected James to come back much earlier than now, and spent many sleepless nights expecting to hear a knock on the door. She had long dreamed of opening that door to see James's huge shoulders at the door, but he was nowhere to be found. She had long since discarded all of her expectations and simply accepted her situation.

James doesn't answer and stares down at the floor for a long moment before looking back up.

"Sage and I are done. I broke up with her last night," James says. He wanted to make the apology a little more dramatic, but he couldn't. That was the best line he could whip out at the moment.

"You did?"

Jenna speaks up, "Wow . . . just like that? I figured you'd need to drive a stake into her heart or something." James hadn't sensed Sage had felt any pain when he broke up with her. Maybe because she had gotten several benefits from the relationship, she had just accepted her fate and moved on.

As he enters the house, Kate puts the sunflowers in a vase. James walks over and takes Kate's hand in his.

"I just wanted to . . ." He could feel his eyes filling up as he fights back the tears while trying to keep his voice steady. "I just wanted both of you to know that the biggest mistake I made in life was losing you. You're the best thing I ever had, and I threw it away for nothing. I had a beautiful family, and I traded it for something I thought I needed."

* * *

Back in the Disco, James suddenly pauses before continuing with his last story.

The Judge opens one eye. "Well, you certainly have had enough time, James . . . Are you going to tell me your true last story or keep me in suspense?

James nodded solemnly. He shut his eyes and leaned toward the microphone while licking his lips. He knew this story would be a nice one; hence, he had to try to make the story interesting to the Judge. The song that was playing now was slow; it had few lyrics but lots of beats.

* * *

"About six months ago, I asked Kate and Jenna Lynn to meet me at our house. Kate's house that is. I had just arrived outside the building."

James is sitting in his car, looking at the guard gate into his old residential community. The engine is off. So is the radio. Alone with his thoughts, he takes a deep breath and opens the car door.

His cell phone buzzes. He looks down, and the caller ID tells him that it's Sage calling. He doesn't answer and sends the call to voicemail instead.

The moment of truth . . .

He looks at the divorce papers in his hands, pauses and then signs them. He then places them into a manila folder. He turns the car back on and drives toward the guard gate.

The guard glances into the car and smiles. "Hey there, Mr. Glass. Haven't seen you around here in a while."

"Could you do me a favor?"

"Sure, Mr. Glass. What do you need?"

He hands the guard the manila folder. "I'm late for a meeting. Could you please drop these off at my . . . ex-wife's house?"

The security guard nods.

James puts the car in reverse and backs away from the development. He pauses, struggling to decide if he has made the right decision or not. He picks up his phone and pulls up Sage's number. He looks from the guard gate back to the phone before he finally dials.

As he hears someone pick up on the other side after a few rings, he says. "Hey baby, it's me. I'm sorry about last night."

James listens to Sage's voice on the other end. Then he says, "Yeah, I'm coming home now."

One last time, James opens his eyes to find himself seated next to the Judge. The Heavenly Judge slowly opens his eyes and exhales as if sipping from a cup of rich coffee.

"I am sad to say that our time together is drawing to a close. I have truly enjoyed it."

The Heavenly Judge reaches out his hand. James stands up to shake it firmly. The Heavenly Judge stares hard at James as if sizing him up. The weight of the moment hangs thick in the air. He begins to feel very nervous. Maybe glad tidings do not await him. James is flooded with doubt and confusion as to his possible fate trying very hard to assess himself before his session with Judge ends.

"I have reached a decision," the Judge says.

There is a long pause as James awaits his final judgment.

"I have taken into account your seven life-changing moments. And my judgment is . . . that you have not earned the right to choose."

The decision hits James like a ton of bricks. He feels deflated and utterly defeated. He feels sad, and a small part of him hopes maybe he will get another chance but deep down there is overwhelming certainty there is no likelihood of that. He looks around; he tries to adjust himself to this horrible, shattering news as he stares into space. Absently, he wonders if he could appeal the judgment. *Is there some sort of form he could request, a court of appeals? Something? Anything?*

The Judge's voice snaps James back to the reality of the moment. "But as I told you, there is one more moment that must be considered. And it shall be the deciding factor."

James begins to feel his heart rate increase in anticipation. *Is there a chance? Is there still hope for him yet?* Like a hero in one of his own films, could he be lucky enough to defeat the odds and win at the last moment?

"Our last action alive can very well determine our fate," the Judge continues. "The problem is that we never know which will be our last action. That is why we must live doing the right thing every day . . . so that if death comes, we will be taken at a good moment."

James recalls his last moment on Earth. He was texting Sage right before his car crashed. He closes his eyes while shaking his head in despair. *No movie ending for him,* James thought, *his luck had run out.*

"Come with me." The Judge starts across the disco floor, heading for the escalators.

James follows. "Wait, I have to ask you something. What's going to happen to Kate?"

The Judge gives him a sideways glance but doesn't answer.

"Come on," James persists, "I mean you have to understand. I need to know if she's going to be okay."

The Judge could see the desperation in his face. "Unfortunately, Kate witnesses the aftermath of your accident."

"She was there?"

"She was arriving at the set. Along with Jenna Lynn."

"My God. What happens . . . after I'm gone?"

"I cannot . . ." The Judge hesitates.

"Please," James begs.

The Judge studies him for a moment. "She does not react well to your passing. Her drinking worsens, her health suffers . . . I am afraid she does not survive the wait for a donor's liver. Jenna Lynn is too wrapped up in her career to make time for her mother. In less than ten years, Kate drinks herself to death. And she dies . . . alone."

"All because of me." James stares into the blazing white spotlights of the disco, momentarily consumed by them. "I know I could change that if I could just tell her . . ."

The Judge cuts him off, "James, everybody wants to go back. But it does not work like that."

James remembers the woman he had seen earlier. He felt that if she could get another chance, then he should still deserve one. Maybe her time was not up and his was.

Suddenly feeling very angry, James snarls at the Judge, "This whole judgment is a joke! If you had ever been alive, if you had a damned heart, you would know that!" He could feel himself on the verge of tears. "You're the last person who should be judging anyone!"

The Judge is silent for a long moment. "I cannot argue your point, James. I can only work with the gift I have been given. To Judge; to the best of my ability." The Judge still seems disinterested about James's fate. He just keeps walking and leaves James without even a stare.

James can only imagine what the Judge will do next. He watches the Judge's finger extend toward two escalators; one going up, one going down. The Judge glances at him. James nods, trying to swallow and having trouble, thanks to the big knot in his throat. He hesitantly walks towards the escalators, face full of fear; the perfect picture of a man terrified of his impending doom.

"Wait!" James is hit with a realization and immediately snaps out of his visualization. "That's it!"

"James?"

"I finally understand it now. The future. What comes next. I've spent my life so worried about it that I forgot to live in the moment and missed out on the now. On the present. Finally."

The Judge begins to smile and nods eagerly for James to continue.

James recalls what has happened in the past. "I was happy with Kate, but I pictured what could be with Whitney. I could have reconciled with Kate, but I imagined Sage and me together. And I looked past my daughter towards personal success, awards, and box office."

"Your mind's eye, your visualizations. That is your gift."

"And also, my curse," James says.

"God provides your talent and gifts, but how you use them is entirely up to you."

"I understand that now. It's time to trust at the moment. And accept it for what it is." James walks towards the escalators and his ultimate fate . . . confident and unconcerned. Satisfied with the outcome. "Thank you for helping me to see that and to understand."

The Judge's cell phone rings.

The Judge glances at the caller ID: Boss.

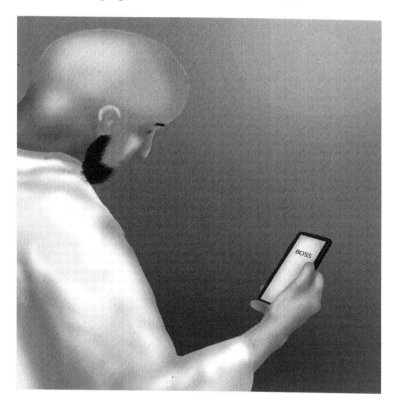

The Judge smiles, "I knew it. His divine love and mercy always find ways to intervene . . ."

The Judge answers the phone, "Yes, Lord?"

As the Judge listens to the caller on the other end, James can feel his eyes on him. James is certain that the call is about him. James is left to silently wonder if his situation is about to get better or worse.

"Yes, it was. That is true . . ." the Judge says. Pausing for a moment, he then says, "Of course."

The Judge then looks over at James, still holding the phone. He glances at the two escalators . . . one up, one down.

"Which one?" James asks.

"Neither. For the moment," the Judge says.

There's a loud ding as an express elevator arrives.

James sees the express elevator, which he had not noticed before, over in the corner of the Disco. The door slides open, waiting. The Judge arches an eyebrow and puts his phone away.

James step inside while asking, "What do I do?"

"Exactly what you just told me. Live in the moment," the Judge replies.

The doors shut.

* * *

Suddenly, James is blinded by a bright white light. He can hear people yelling and sirens approaching.

James opens his eyes wide, and he can see from the corner of his eyes, broken glass and shattered pieces of the taillight. He suddenly feels immense pain all over his body as wet trickles of blood run over his face. James notices Kate and Jenna Lynn by his side, cradling his head. They are both in tears.

"Hang on, James. Just hang on," Kate wails.

James tries talking, finds that he can and isn't about to miss this blessed opportunity. "Kate . . . Jenna Lynn . . . I'm sorry . . ." He finds the strength to continue. "I just wanted you to know that the biggest mistake I made in my life was losing you. You guys are the best thing I ever had, and I threw it away."

Kate says, "James, you have to . . ."

James interrupts her. "It is all my fault; I wasn't the husband or the father you deserved." James can feel Kate squeeze his hand. Surprisingly, his body relaxes even in the face of all the stress and pain. The squeezing signals that she is okay with him and has now forgiven him. She is trying very hard to make him understand that she forgives him, hoping that will help drive him to fight to stay alive.

"Just hold on," Kate tries to reassure him.

James struggles to look around. Jenna Lynn is a mess; half in shock, tears flowing . . .

"Dad!" she screams. Jenna Lynn is in pain seeing her father like this. Her only hope in this moment is that she will be able to hug him again, sit around him and joke with him about *who is more popular* like they used to do. But she isn't certain that there is enough time.

James can feel himself fading. "I hope one day you can both forgive me . . . I . . . love . . . you . . . ."

Rick pulls up on a golf cart. The little kid who wants to be a director one day sits next to him, on his tour of the set. His mom is in the back of the golf cart and covers his eyes to protect him from seeing the blood. He's still wearing James's ball cap.

James can hear Rick say to them, "Stay here."

"Rick! Oh, my God!" Kate screams.

Rick tries to reassure Kate, "The ambulance is right behind me." He knows that it is a futile mission, yet he still spills out words of hope and encouragement.

Tears and anguish fill Kate's smooth face.

* * *

In the Disco room, the Judge looks at the multimedia screens.

The Judge is intently watching the scene transpire on the screen. He is ready to pull the plug on James, but he waits . . . He listens to his headphones and surprises even himself that he does so with a face full of emotion. For the first time, the Judge feels something, and though it is fleeting, it is truly wonderful. *Is this how they feel all the time?* the Judge suddenly wonders. *Amazing.* He tries to give James a few moments so he can make things okay with his family.

Faith looks at him oddly, but he waves her off.

"This is one of my favorite songs. I'm just sad when it's over."

The paramedics arrive and slide James onto a stretcher, securing him in a neck brace to immobilize his head. They administer an IV into his arm. He leans his head back on the stretcher while staring up toward Heaven. He closes his eyes and smiles. He is finally at peace...

The paramedics desperately try to save him...the lights of the ambulance flash red and white.

Those flashing lights fade away and make way for the lights of the Disco.

The elevator door opens, and James stumbles out.

The Judge is there to catch James as he is dazed and struggling to keep upright. He blinks as tears track down his cheeks.

"Was that . . . I mean, did all that happen?" James asks. "Or did I just visualize how I wanted it to . . ."

"I can assure you everything you did was real."

"Then, thank you . . . Thank you so much! Is Kate going to be okay now?"

"I will not see Kate for a long time. You did it, James." The Judge smiles. "You got your Director's Cut."

"I'm grateful, but I don't understand how." James tries to comprehend how everything has played out and why he was gifted with a second chance, there at the end.

The Judge reaches out and touches James's forehead. They both share the same visualization.

James's phone rings. He looks down and does not accept Sage's call. He smiles, reaches up, and takes off his ball cap to plop it on the kid's head.

Back in the Disco, the Judge nods toward him.

"You have demonstrated the remorse in your heart. And you have also finally learned not to surrender to greed, and to lend a hand to others not as fortunate. And the boy will always remember your kindness. Inspiring him to achieve his dream of being a director. And the movies he makes shall further inspire others and bring many people closer to God."

"The final moment."

"That is why every moment should be lived like it was the last." James had been taught this while he was growing up.

"I'm ready to go now."

The Judge extends his finger toward the up escalator. James smiles, having finally found peace in his heart.

"Now do I get to choose who I . . ." James asks. James stammers as he asks the question and tries to see if the decision of the Judge could change and allow him to choose whom he will be with in heaven.

"You already have."

The Judge and James make eye contact even as he is carried upwards.

The Judge gives a curt nod. James nods back and gives a small wave as he is carried up and away into a blinding white light.

* * *

Thirty years, thirty days or thirty seconds later,

Fate is speaking to an elderly Hispanic woman. The endless list in front of her grows longer by the second.

"Hola. Mi nombre es Fate."

"Te estábamos esperando. Escalera eléctrica ... Piso número treinta."

The woman takes the escalator and goes slowly to floor number thirty.

The Judge looks at the woman coming in, and he says: "Have a seat Cristina, and speak without concern. There is only one language here, and we all can understand it and can speak it fluently."

The woman was happily surprised and says, "Is this the final judgment or something?"

"Yes," the Judge says, "but first I need to listen to seven important moments of your life to evaluate if you choose your future or if I decide your future, which won't be a very pleasant situation.

"Oh my God, help me!" the woman says. "I am a nurse, and I have helped a lot of people!!"

"Cristina," the Judge says, "go ahead and start your stories." If only Cristina knew that her stories would determine her eternity. She has a bit of a sad look with a lot of pity written over her face. She wears a pink medical gown that makes her look very young.

"Ok, sir," Cristina says.

"My husband Carlos and I grew up in the same neighborhood; it was a poor area, but decent and friendly. We went to the same schools, but neither of us was able to go to college. We didn't have such great grades, and our parents didn't have enough money to pay for college."

Realizing she is talking fast because she is so nervous, Cristina takes a deep breath to calm herself down. She feels like she is at a job interview. *No, this is much more important,* she thinks. Cristina laughs to herself at the absurdity of the situation and continues: "When we got married, we moved away to a better area, but it seems the better the houses look, the colder and more distant people become. We had two children that grew nicely, we went to church every Sunday, and we helped others."

"Carlos had a job in construction with good pay, and he was always busy. We had most everything we wanted and more. But one day, my husband fell from a high rise and died."

"That's a story of triumph and sadness," says the Judge, "Tell me the next story."

And so, Cristina went on, "When my husband died, we got some money from insurance he had on his job that helped us for a few years. But the time came where I decided I needed to work and reluctantly started working in a nursing home, as a nursing assistant. At the beginning it was hard for me to see elderly people in their last stages of life and try to bathe, feed, dress them, and even provide them with company since most family members didn't visit with them.

"It was a frustrating and difficult job until I met George, a resident that lived there with no visits from family. He had a nasty attitude and liked to scream and make demands. I was assigned to George for a few days and took care of him as my job required. The following week I was assigned to other residents and was not assigned to George."

"Suddenly another assistant came to me and said, 'George is asking why you are not taking care of him today. I told him you were assigned to other residents, and he says he won't eat or take a shower if you don't go see him.'"

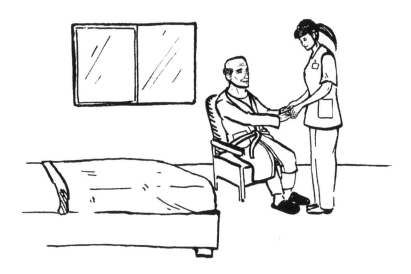

"I went to see George, and he was very upset.

Why have you left me?' he said.

"I tried to explain to him how they make the assignments. And he didn't want to hear it. He wanted me. And if I didn't feed him, he wouldn't eat, or bathe, or anything.

"It happened that I spoke with the Director of Nurses, and she assigned me to take care of George every day that I worked. And I did." She pauses, wiping her face as if some sweat had gathered on her forehead before continuing. Her eyes fix on the Judge as she tells her stories. It makes more look more sincere. The Judge listens with rapt attention as she continues.

"When I took days off, George was upset, and it took me a long time for him to understand that I needed to take time off to be with my own family.

"You see, George had no family. I was his family. He smiled to see me. I smile back at him when I see him.

"George made me realize the immense job of caring for the elderly. And I came to love it. I went to school to become a Registered Nurse because I wanted to dedicate myself to the care of the elderly. I lost a family member when George died a couple of years later."

* * *

In the Heavenly Lounge, the bank of clocks on the wall keeps ticking away. All around the lounge, people amuse themselves by reading or playing games while they wait.

There are pool tables, darts, and even a basketball hoop. James is busy playing basketball with a group. He is excited that he just scored and keeps running back and forth on defense.

* * *

"Hello. My name is Fate. We've been expecting you. Your hand, please."

After a moment of confusion, the woman presents her outstretched hand

And Fate stamps the hand with a familiar number, thirty.

Kate, now thirty-three, of course, looks down at the stamp then back up at Fate, a bit confused.

"The show is about to start. And you certainly don't want to be late. Take the escalator at the end of that hall, please. The one that goes up. For now."

Back in the Disco:

"After all your stories, I have decided . . ." the Judge says, adding a dramatic pause, "you can choose who you will be with in Heaven."

"Oh, thank you, Lord, thank you," Cristina says. "I want to be with Carlos, my husband. He must be waiting for me."

"Yes," the Judge says, "he is waiting for you, and you will go now to see him."

"That's great, sir. I'd love to see him."

"Sir, can I ask you a question?"

"Sure, Cristina," responds the Judge.

"Can I see George also? I'd love to stop and say hello."

The Judge smiles, saying, "Yes, Cristina, you will see him, he is waiting for you also. Now take the elevator up. Just push the button, and it will take you to your destination."

And as Cristina gets into the elevator, the Judge goes to the console and turns on a very nice and smooth tune. Picks up his cell phone and says, "Fate, I am ready for the next one . . ."

* * *

A very nervous Kate rides the escalator until she sees floor number thirty and walks into the disco.

The Judge is already waiting for her.

"Have a seat, Kate, and welcome to the final judgment. Tell me seven stories of the most important moments in your life and . . ."

Kate sits down across from the Heavenly Judge. She looks around bewildered, trying to take everything in, hardly able to believe what she is seeing. She tries to focus on what the Judge is saying:

". . . if the majority are good, you shall pick with whom you spend eternity in Heaven. If the majority are bad, then Kate, I will choose your fate."

The Judge leans back in his chair, fingers steepled under his chin as he studies Kate.

Kate is so nervous. She doesn't know how to start, looks around the disco, the console, and then she gets herself together and starts speaking:

"I was very excited when I met my first love. He was running away from the security guard at the school when he sat beside me to hide with the newspaper I was reading. The encounter struck me so much that in the evening, I prayed to meet him again. It was not an easy thing either since he was a senior and I was a freshman."

As she recalls the moment, her voice still quivers, reliving the excitement of the long past moment, "To my surprise and joy the next day, I saw when he dropped his film while jumping onto the roof."

"I said to myself, 'my prayers are answered. There is a chance.' I picked up his roll of film. I had his life in my hands. I saw him that day, and we kissed." Her cheeks blush red at the memory. "From that moment on, he had my life in his hands."

The Judge looks at Kate and says, "Seems to me I heard a similar story, but keep going . . ."

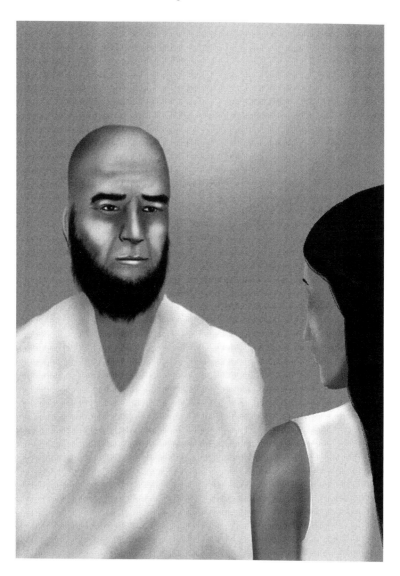

Kate looks surprised and wonders what he means but continues. "We got married after he graduated, and I continued school for a couple of years. He worked on several movie productions, and by the time I graduated, he was directing a low budget film before working for a big production studio in Los Angeles."

"We were very happy. We supported each other; we loved each other; we liked each other. James always said our life was going to be a sixty-year-long movie produced by us, together

"When my painting was not successful, he always said to keep trying, that I have the talent, and the time would come when people would recognize it."

"When he kept expecting to get awards and didn't get nominated or win them, I always said, keep trying, you have the talent. The Academy will recognize you sooner or later."

"And on top of all the blessings was Jenna Lynn. The joy of our family. We were a very happy family for a few years. But I wanted to have another baby, and the doctors said I couldn't. We saw many doctors looking for answers, and they all said I couldn't. I became frustrated and started drinking more than socially. James started to come home late more often. I started to think he was with another woman. I made an effort and tried so hard to stop drinking to focus on saving my marriage, but by then it was too late.

* * *

James is in the game, dribbling the basketball and looking to get open to make the shot. Something catches his attention . . . he looks up and sees Kate as she hesitantly enters the Heavenly Lounge. She walks around searching the lounge and approaches the stands of the basketball court.

The Heavenly Judge's phone rings. "Yes, My Lord..." he says while he listens.

"Oh . . . no, I cannot do it. It has to be you. Only you have that Supreme Power."

When he hangs up, he says, "Thy will be done."

The Judge sets his headphones in place and plays his song.

"I need some live music for this one!" Maybe I will go to the Sunset Festival in Key West.

James's eyes widen. He smiles, the basketball falls from his hands . . .

Kate runs over to James, and they embrace and begin to kiss desperately.

And the two of them are laughing as they fly in a convertible through the sky, James's hand on the gearshift and Kate's hand over his. The wind whips her hair around her face. James beams at her.

"We'll be together forever," James says.

His convertible speeds away into the sunset, disappearing into the horizon. They vanish into eternity together. They both had the familiar touch they needed.

Snapping from his visualization, Kate smiles and walks toward James. But she doesn't stop. She just keeps walking past James with her eyes on someone else as she continues walking.

James is devastated at that moment. He grabs the basketball, hurls it with all his might toward the net, and screams.

"Noooooo! My Lord, my God, My Superhero!!!"

The ball strikes the backboard, bounces off the rim of the basket with a flat gonging sound, and then starts floating upward into the sky.

Up, up, and away. The orange ball vibrates with power until it no longer is a basketball in mid-air. It is simply a sphere, in its truest form, carrying with it an untold amount of energy. The sphere streaks up through the atmosphere and into the star-filled sky, trailing fire behind it like a blazing comet. It glows brightly, pulsing with an inner light, as it speeds into the field of stars and transforms into something else . . . becoming the sun.

* * *

All of a sudden, time starts reversing, the sun rises from the western horizon and cuts an unnatural swath through the clouds. The sun becomes a full glorious moon becomes the sun again as the days cycle backward, everything moving faster as the rotation turns into a blur.

Reality becomes like a rock tied upon the end of a string being swung by a child. It spins faster and faster until it ceases being just one solid thing and appears everywhere it travels along the blur of its own path, Transforms into its own orbit. A singe beautiful fusion of matter and motion.

The seasons run backward; winter to fall, to summer, and then to spring. The snow retreats up into the cool autumn sky and what is left is instantly melted by the blazing sun, as crops and flowers recede into the ground.

A horse gallops along a field. Bits of grass and dirt shower the trail behind the panting animal, driven by its thundering hooves. Then, as time recedes, the beast grows smaller and smaller, its long stride shrinking as it becomes a young colt.

A towering pine tree, rising a hundred feet off the forest floor, with its trunk thickened like a football player. The green glory grows smaller and smaller; the trunk shrinks in upon itself, its thick branches withdrawing unusually quickly as if they frightened of something. In the span of a few eyeblinks, it becomes merely a sapling tree again.

An adult man walks along, tall and bulky and well-muscled. The wrinkles on his face vanish as his skin smooths out. His thinning hair returns to its lush fullness as his strong frame shrinks down to half its size. The man finally returns to innocence as he reverses the stages of life all the way to infancy, crawling on hands and knees, babbling his way toward the splendor of a rising sun.

Time reverses and reverses, like a great cosmic rewind button has been pressed. The moments of life increase in speed, moving faster and faster, racing everything else in existence and winning easily. Time streaks past the lumbering speed of sound, like the hare rocketing past the tortoise in a race. The sound cannot hope to keep pace, and everything and anything that can be heard in nature is nothing but a jumble of white noise.

Until time finally slows down, tired from the remarkable effort, and then sound catches up. And noise slowly resolves itself into a single thrilling sound everyone can recognize: the droning, echoing wail of an ambulance siren.

Kate is inside the back of the ambulance, her hand on James. A female ambulance paramedic huddles over him, attending to his medical needs. Suddenly, James awakens and screams:

"My Lord! My Superhero! Please! I want to be with Kate in Heaven!"

Kate strokes his forehead; tears roll down her cheeks.

"Oh my God, James! Yes, yes. But not yet, baby. We're going to have a long life together first. I love you so much."

James is disoriented for a minute. Like when you jolt awake and have no idea where you are or what time it is. Then he focuses on Kate and calms down. "I love you, Kate," he says.

Kate hugs him as best she can, and James closes his eyes for a moment, breathing in her hair, her smell.

When James opens his eyes again, something immediately draws his attention. He knows he will recognize her somehow . . . The female paramedic . . . A familiar face! She looks like . . . Just like...

"Fate!" James exclaims.

"No, my name is Salvacion, sir."

James looks from her to Kate. "Honey, what is she doing here?"

"James, she's your savior! She arrived just in time. Relax, my love."

James looks closely at the paramedic named Salvacion. This time her face is different, no longer the same as Fate. The subtle switch happens so fast, faster than the eye can follow.

James opens his eyes and smiles.

As if he was *visualizing or thinking*:

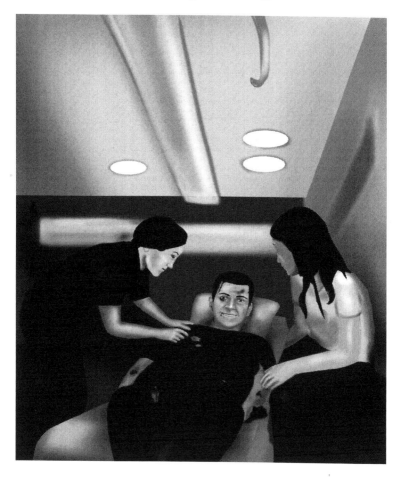

"Hello. My name is Fate. We've been expecting you..."